Can't resist a sexy military hero?
*Then you'll love our **Uniformly Hot!** miniseries.*

Harlequin Blaze's bestselling miniseries
continues with more irresistible heroes
from all branches of the armed forces.

Don't miss

WICKED SECRETS
by Anne Marsh
April 2015

A SEAL'S PLEASURE
by Tawny Weber
May 2015

FEVERED NIGHTS
by Jillian Burns
June 2015

Dear Reader,

On the surface, *Search and Seduce* is a sexy romance about a smoking-hot solider, a strong military widow who is trying to find her way, and puppies bred to be war dogs. But beyond the red-hot moments, the Air Force Pararescueman who looks yummy in and out of uniform, and the adorable canines, this is a story about what it means to be a military wife, girlfriend and widow. And I sincerely hope that part resonates with readers. Every day brave military partners face the fear of not knowing if the person they love is in danger. They wait day after day for their partners to come home, knowing they will leave again. In telling Amy and Mark's story, I tried to offer a window into their world—and give two very brave characters a heartfelt happily-ever-after ending.

And, of course, I hope you love the puppies! Thank you to my Facebook fans for suggesting names for Amy's dogs. Your ideas were excellent and I used many of them in the book. As I said in the dedication, this one is for you!

As my Facebook friends know, I love hearing from readers! Please find me on Facebook or drop by my website, sarajanestone.com. And while you're there don't forget to sign up for my newsletter to receive information about new releases, contests and more.

Happy reading!

Sara Jane Stone

Sara Jane Stone

Search and Seduce

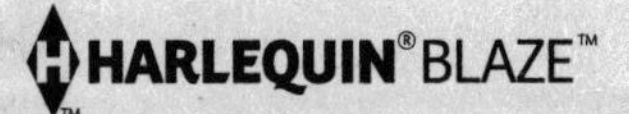

ISBN-13: 978-0-373-79839-1

Search and Seduce

This edition published by arrangement with Harlequin Books S.A.

For questions and comments about the quality of this book, please contact us at CustomerService@Harlequin.com.

Printed in U.S.A.

Sara Jane Stone lives in Brooklyn, New York, with her very supportive real-life hero, two lively young children and a lazy Burmese cat. When she is not finger painting with the kids, she loves writing sexy stories featuring military heroes (and heroines!), reading sexy contemporary romance and chatting with her readers. Visit her online at sarajanestone.com, and become a fan of Sara Jane Stone on Facebook.

Books by Sara Jane Stone

HARLEQUIN BLAZE

Command Performance
Command Control

To get the inside scoop on Harlequin Blaze and its talented writers, be sure to check out blazeauthors.com.

All backlist available in ebook format.

Visit the Author Profile page at Harlequin.com for more titles

For my Facebook friends and fans. Thank you for helping me name the puppies! This one is for you and I hope to see you online again soon.

And to my husband, I love you!

Prologue

SAILORS, SOLDIERS AND AIRMEN lined the grave site. Amy Benton stared at them, noting the differences in their dress uniforms. The men in the dark blues stood at attention beside the ones in the bright whites. Medals lined their chests, every single one.

These men were Darren's brothers, teammates and friends. And their presence here, at her husband's grave, made the truth undeniable. Darren, the man she'd fallen head over heels in love with more than a decade ago, back when they were high school students, was not coming home again.

Her chin dropped to her chest. Freshly shined shoes stood in sharp contrast to the bright green grass. She looked at her scuffed black flats, drawing her lower lip into her mouth. She'd forgotten to polish her shoes.

Amy's hands formed tight fists, her pale pink nails digging into her palms as the tears threatened. She'd painted her fingernails. That had to count for something. But how could she forget about her shoes?

Maybe she'd worn the wrong pair. She tried to think back to this morning, but the hours blurred together. She felt as if she'd spent a series of endless days, unable to sleep, fighting her way through a sea of pain, allowing herself to bury the truth.

Standing here in her scuffed shoes, she couldn't hide anymore.

But falling apart surrounded by these men in their pristine uniforms? Impossible. Biting back her sobs, she closed her eyes, fighting the urge to run. That wasn't her. She didn't draw attention. Darren's place was in the spotlight—and hers was waiting off to the side with a smile plastered on her face.

Once upon a time that smile had been real. Slowly, it had become something she wore only when leaving the house, not much different from a hat. And then she'd lost it altogether. It was as if she'd set it aside the day those strangers in uniform had knocked on her door, their expressions lined with pity. She'd put her smile in a closet and closed the door.

Damn him for leaving her to face this alone!

Opening her eyes, Amy turned away from the burial. She couldn't do this, couldn't watch. She moved toward the trees, unsure where she was going. Away. From his death and the seemingly insurmountable, endless pain.

She stumbled over a root. A man's hand grasped her elbow, steadying her.

"I've got you." The familiar voice was a low steady rumble.

"I can't go back," she whispered. "I can't."

"You don't have to." Mark Rhodes, her husband's best friend since grade school, kept a hold on her arm, leading her away.

The tears came, hot and fast, so far beyond her control, she didn't try to hold them back. Mark stopped beside her car, gently leaning her against the passenger-side door while he reached in his pocket and withdrew a key.

"I'm taking you home," he said.

Amy nodded, allowing him to guide her into the seat and fasten her belt. She should protest, ask him to drive to her mother-in-law's house, where the family, friends and all those men in uniform planned to congregate after the burial. But she didn't say a word.

Mark drove in silence. He didn't demand to know how she was feeling—though it was probably obvious from her tears—or offer reassurances. When they pulled up to her house, he helped her out of the car as if she were a child.

Taking her hand, he led her away from the front door and down through the grass. Out back, only a short distance from the home she'd shared with Darren, stood her kennel. It was a modest building capable of boarding a dozen pets. At the moment, it stood empty. Her customers had all come for their dogs to give her the time and space to grieve.

But right now, she wanted to hear barking. She craved the sounds of everyday life.

Mark guided her to a wooden bench beside the dog run, a large fenced-in area.

"Sit down, Amy," he said, tempering his command with a gentle tone as if she were a frightened animal.

Amy obeyed, staring out at the mountains in the distance. Heart's Landing, Oregon, her home since birth, sat a few miles inland from the coast, surrounded by distant mountains. She loved this view and this place. But not today.

"I wish I'd worn ruby slippers," she said.

Mark sat down beside her on the bench. Out of the

corner of her eye, she saw him glance at her black flats. "Might have looked out of place."

She shook her head. "Ruby slippers so that I could click my heels three times and disappear."

"Dorothy went home. She didn't vanish," he pointed out. "And the loss would follow you."

Her brow drew together as she studied him for the first time since he'd helped her run away from the burial. Like so many of the other men, Mark wore his dress blues. The maroon beret on his head set him apart from the others, denoting that he was a member of the Air Force Pararescuemen. But beneath his uniform and his elite status, she saw her friend, the man who'd been a part of her life from the moment she'd met Darren.

"There's no escape?" If anyone would give her the truth, it was Mark.

"From grief?" He took her hand and held it tight. "No."

"But you look so calm and in control. You know Darren's gone, right? He's never coming back."

"I know, Amy. Trust me, I understand what it feels like to face the irrefutable fact that someone you love is gone."

This time when she examined his expression, she saw the sadness, swirling in his brown eyes. "Your mom," she said quietly. "How did you get past it?"

"I tried to escape. Moving away, joining the air force, pushing myself to complete the courses and become a pararescue jumper. But it stayed with me."

"Nothing helped?"

"Time." He stared out at the scenery. "And I started a list."

"Of what?"

"Memories. I wrote down the little moments, the pieces I didn't want to forget."

"A list," she said as if she didn't understand the meaning of the words. How could something so simple, so banal, ease this monstrous ache?

Mark shrugged. "It might not work for you. But I can tell you ruby slippers won't do the trick, either."

"I'll give it a shot." She couldn't stay here forever, unable to eat and sleep, feeling lost in her own life. If she didn't do something…

Tears started flowing again. She hiccuped, struggling to control the sobs as her chin shook.

Mark wrapped an arm around her shoulder and drew her close. "I'll tell you what, write down your memories and send them to me. Write a letter or email. Send a carrier pigeon if you want. Whatever you need to share. Every small memory matters. And I'll do the same, send my favorite Darren moments to you."

"Do you have a memory at the top of your list?" Her voice sounded foreign, still trembling from her latest bout of crying.

"Not yet," he said, and for the first time she heard his calm and collected tone waver.

Amy looped her arm around his waist, holding him tight as they stared out at the mountains, both thinking about the man they'd loved and lost.

"Mark," she said softly. "Not all of my memories are good ones."

"That's okay, Amy. That's okay."

1

One year later

"SCRAMBLE. SCRAMBLE."

The commander's voice echoed through the tactical operations center's loudspeakers. Mark Rhodes leaned over the intel officer's shoulder and scanned the details on the computer screen. IED blast. Double amputee. American. Special Forces. He ran for the door.

When he'd first joined the PJs, if he'd heard a mission drop, fear would have settled in his gut. What if their helicopter got hit? What if they landed on a mine? Sure, they touched down in swept areas, but shit happened. In Kandahar Province, Afghanistan, it happened every day.

But now, on his fourth deployment, he wanted to get out there and do his job. Save a life. Send a soldier home to his loved ones.

Mark reached the helicopter and started pulling on his gear. "One Alpha," he shouted to his teammates over the bird's roar. "This guy needs a hospital within the hour. And we're going in hot. We're picking him up outside the wire."

His team nodded and climbed into the bird. They went to work, prepping IVs, getting ready to do whatever they could to keep the fallen soldier alive.

"How long has he been down?" one of Mark's teammates asked as they lifted into the air.

"Twenty, based on when the call came in," Mark said. By the time they reached the soldier, they would have only minutes to get him in the air and to a hospital. After one hour, the guy's chances of making it dropped significantly.

Minutes later, Mark's lead helicopter landed, leaving the trail helo circling overhead to provide cover. When the dust settled, three men carrying a stretcher emerged, running toward Mark and his team. They loaded the injured American on board. The soldier was conscious, a good sign. But he'd lost a lot of blood.

"Let's go," Mark shouted into his headset, then turned to his teammate. "Start an IO, this guy needs blood." Drilling into the man's arm and sending the blood directly to the bone was their best shot. Still, Mark added, "Prep an IV as backup."

The solider turned his head toward Mark. His lips moved. Mark took the injured man's hand and leaned over, pressing his ear close to the guy's mouth.

"Repeat that," Mark said.

"I wish I'd told her I loved her," the injured soldier whispered. "My girl."

"Stay with me and you'll get your chance."

"Not this time, man." The soldier's eyes fluttered, then closed. The hand Mark was holding went limp.

"We're losing him." Mark pressed his fingers to the soldier's neck, searching for a pulse. It was there. Barely. Dammit, at times like this, he wished he'd gone to medical school and had the skills to open the guy up. But even the best surgeon probably couldn't do more than Mark and his team in the back of a helicopter flying over a war zone.

His teammate, hovering over what was left of the man's legs, shook his head. "This is bad. He's lost a lot of blood."

"How far are we from the hospital?" Mark spoke into his headset, hoping like hell the pilot said five minutes or less.

"Wheels down in fifteen. Maybe more. There are reports of enemy fire to the east. We need to take the long way around."

Shit. They couldn't risk getting shot out of the sky, but this guy didn't have fifteen.

"Starting CPR." Mark checked for a pulse again. Nothing. They were losing him. Fast. He began compressions on the guy's chest.

Twenty minutes later the bird was still in the air, taking the goddamn scenic route to avoid rocket launchers, and the soldier still didn't have a pulse. They'd lost him. Mark knew it. But he refused to give up. He continued CPR until the helicopter touched down.

On the ground, Mark and his teammates rode with the soldier in the ambulance. He ran alongside his stretcher as they wheeled him into the trauma bay, conveying every detail to the doctors. But he knew that look in their eyes. The doctors were good, but they couldn't save him now.

Mark stood, his teammates beside him, watching and waiting. What felt like an eternity later, after they'd tried everything they could, the attending called it.

His teammate stepped forward and handed Mark a

folded American flag, one of the ones they prepped during their downtime at the base. He carried it forward and laid it on the fallen soldier's chest, and then he turned and walked away.

They did their best to honor fallen soldiers. But it wasn't enough. It was never enough. Somewhere, half a world away, this man had a family and friends who had no idea they'd just lost their loved one.

And this guy—he had a girl.

Mark climbed into the helicopter for the ride back to base and closed his eyes. He hoped the soldier was wrong. He hoped the man's girl knew how he felt about her.

But if she did know, when she learned of his death, her world would shatter. And picking up the pieces wasn't easy. Sometimes he still felt as if the wind had been knocked out of him when he thought about losing his best friend. And he'd watched Darren's widow navigate her own pain. Witnessing her struggle, especially in those early months, was hard.

Mark opened his eyes and stared out the window, watching the colorless landscape speed by beneath the helo. As much as he missed his mom, part of him was glad she'd already passed away. If a rocket launcher hit this helicopter right now, if tomorrow he took a bullet trying to save a fellow solider, he wouldn't leave behind someone deeply bound to his memory. He couldn't do that to someone he loved. And loving him—the kid who'd grown up with nothing, whose father had never given him a second thought and whose mother had worked two jobs just to get by—wasn't worth the pain of losing him.

Back at base, the helicopter touched down, and Mark

headed for the barracks. He needed to wash up and check his gear. In twelve hours, he had to be prepared to go out there again and risk his life to save a life.

The alarm on Mark's watch sounded. He glanced down and checked the time. Shit. He was late for his video chat with Amy, the one person he made an effort to keep in touch with back home. He picked up the pace.

"Hey, Mark, time for your date?" Tommy, the team rookie, joked.

"It's not a date," he said gruffly, jogging past his teammates.

"You talk to that chick every week. She must be giving you something."

"Show some respect," Mark said. "She's a widow. Her husband was my friend. When he got hit, he had less of a chance than the guy we lost today."

Tommy sobered instantly. "Sorry, man."

Mark nodded, apology accepted, as he pushed through the door. In the break room, Mark opened his laptop, the one he'd quickly set aside when the mission had dropped. While he waited for it to connect, he glanced down. Blood covered his shirt. No way he could talk to Amy like this. He pulled it over his head and tossed it aside.

"Mark?" Amy's soft voice filled the quiet space followed by her image on the screen. She held a cup of coffee in her hands, her blond hair loose and flowing over her shoulders. When she was out working with her dogs, she always tied it back, tucking her long bangs behind her ears. But it was early still in Oregon, not even six in the morning. He knew she woke up hours before the sun every Sunday for this call.

Keeping in touch and maintaining their friendship

meant something to her. Even though part of him wanted to sever ties with everyone back home, he couldn't let go of Amy. She'd already lost so much, burying her husband at twenty-eight. If there was anything he could do to help her, he would.

For months after Darren's funeral, they'd played the memory game, writing up long lists and sending them back and forth. She reminded him of some of the best parts of growing up in Heart's Landing. She'd made him laugh, and once or twice, her list had reduced him to tears.

"I'm here." He studied the screen. Amy kept her computer on her kitchen table. Through the window behind her, he could usually see Oregon's coastal range. But today, on an early October morning, it was too dark. Part of him missed those mountains and the smell of the ocean in the air.

Mark turned his attention back to Amy, taking in the dark circles under her blue eyes. He forced a smile. For her sake, he put on a front, trying to be the fun-loving guy she remembered, not the jaded solider. "Amelia Mae, you look exhausted. Are you sleeping?"

"Hmm?" She drew her lower lip between her teeth, running her tongue back and forth, her gaze fixed on his bare chest. She hadn't even noticed his smile. She'd been staring at his muscles. Maybe she was reading the words tattooed across his pecs—*so that others may live.* Or maybe she was just plain looking.

And that look, combined with the way she nibbled on her lower lip, swirling her tongue as if she wanted to taste, maybe touch, spoke to part of his body that had no business participating in their weekly chat.

Hell, this was Amy. But one more second of that

look and he'd freaking *want* her. Every beautiful, blond inch of her.

Mark closed his eyes, pushing the thought away. He couldn't go there. And dammit, he should have taken the time to find a clean shirt. He'd loved Amy for years, but never in a let's-get-naked way. They'd been friends since high school. Nothing more. Not a chance.

Still, he wasn't blind. Amy was gorgeous. But wanting what he couldn't have…he knew better.

"What happened to your shirt?" she asked, finally looking up at his face.

"Bad day."

"You lost someone," she said softly.

"American. Special Forces." She didn't need to know the details, to picture the man bleeding out in the helicopter. He'd probably already said too much. Amy's husband had been a SEAL. Darren had died over a year ago, but Mark knew the grief still weighed heavily on her.

"I'm sorry."

He nodded. What was there to say? He was sorry, too.

"You can talk to me, Mark. I'm here and I'm listening."

"Are you trying to make me tear up?" he said, forcing a lightness he didn't feel, not by a long shot.

"We can joke and laugh if you want. But if you need to get it off your chest—"

"He'd lost both legs. Bled out in the helicopter. We couldn't get him to a hospital in time. It sucked. Just plain sucked." He rubbed his hands over his face. He'd been kidding about crying, but now he wasn't so sure.

"We can wait and talk next week," she said. "If you need to clean up. Rest."

"No, my shift's over, and I've been looking forward

to catching up. The shower will still be waiting for me when we're done," he said. "But I can grab a shirt."

She shook her head. "No. Don't worry about it. I was just...surprised."

There was a long pause. Mark wondered if the screen had frozen. But then Jango, the dog that had served with his best friend, appeared in the background. The Belgian Malinois was technically retired after years of working alongside navy SEALs, sniffing for bombs and weapons in war zones, but Jango didn't act like a senior citizen adjusting to a life of chasing balls. Years of training, combined with natural instincts, might always prevent the dog from relaxing. Instead, Jango followed Amy as if she was his new handler.

Mark cleared his throat. "In your email, you said you had something to tell me. Big news."

"I do. And you're the first one outside of family to know about this." Her face lit up like a kid's on Christmas morning, and he damn near fell off the couch. He hadn't seen her that excited in years.

"I'm opening a military war dog breeding and training facility. It will mean shutting down my current K-9 training business and remodeling the kennels, but in the end, it will be worth it." Amy spoke quickly, her fingers drumming the side of her coffeecup. "Darren's mother and his brothers support the idea. In fact, they're donating a few acres of their land. I'll be able to expand the training grounds and, in time, build another kennel. If I have the funds.

"The Department of Defense offered preliminary approval. They have their own breeding programs, but they'll buy my pups, too. Provided the dogs fit with what they're looking for. And they will. I've already bought a pair of Belgian Malinois from Denmark, both from top bloodlines. In the past, the DOD has been sending someone over there to purchase puppies. Now they will be born and receive their basic training right here in Oregon."

She paused and lifted her coffee to her lips, then lowered it. "So, what do you think?"

"It's great."

For the first time in months, Amy sparkled. She looked like her old self again. Sure, turning her business into a military war dog program sounded cool, but she could have told him she was joining the circus, and he would have supported her 100 percent if it made her this happy.

"One more thing," she said. Was it his imagination or had the light in her eyes dimmed? Shit, maybe she'd been looking for more enthusiasm. This was huge for her—a way to move on with her life. And he wanted that for her.

"I'm planning to open in three months and hold a dedication a few months later, probably in early March, when some of Darren's brothers are expected home for a visit," she continued. "Nothing big. Just family and friends. Maybe a few members of the community who express interest. Do you think you can come? You can stay in the spare bedroom."

Heart's Landing wasn't a place he'd planned to visit during his brief time stateside. But the thought of seeing Amy again, in person, pushed against his reservations. This time, when he returned to his hometown, it would be for her, 100 percent. She was his closest friend now. And if there was anything he could do to help her, he was on board.

"I'm done here around then. So, yeah, I'll be there," he said. "You can count on it."

2

Five months later

BLOND HAIR TRAILED over his bare chest. She kissed his stomach, moving lower...

"Amy." Her name was a plea. "Amy."

"Hey, Rhodes." The familiar sound of his teammate's voice silenced his dream. "Better wake up, man, before you embarrass yourself. I don't know who 'Amy' is, but she sure as hell isn't here."

Mark opened his eyes, blinking. What the hell? He was on a freaking plane over the ocean, still a helluva long way from Heart's Landing and the wild, sexy woman in his dream. Amy. Except Amy had never been wild. She was quiet, always holding back. At least in high school. They'd had that in common.

Of course, he'd changed, and she probably had, too. But it didn't matter if she'd taken up pole dancing now that she was single; she wasn't for him.

"Yeah, crazy dream, man," Mark said. "But it's not what you think."

Thinking about Amy like that, dreaming about her…

Guilt rose up, wrapping around him, adding to the weight on his shoulders.

"Could have fooled me." His teammate shook his head, picking up his book.

Mark looked out the window. He didn't need to fool his fellow PJs. Just Amy and everyone else in Heart's Landing.

AMY STOOD OUTSIDE the remodeled kennel holding an empty dog food dish and waiting for her cousin. A very hungry Belgian Malinois sat at her feet.

She stole a quick peek through the glass-paned door into the reception area. Three men gathered around the box of doughnuts and coffee she'd set out on the folding table. The food had bought her a five-minute delay, ten tops. But leaving three soldiers waiting was like placing puppies in the living room and expecting them to keep their mouths off the furniture. As soon as the doughnuts disappeared, the guys would become restless. They wouldn't chew the chair legs, but they'd get into something.

If Eloise didn't get here soon—

"You are the only person in the whole world I would drop everything for to deliver a ten-pound bag of gluten-free dog food."

Amy stepped back from the door and turned to her cousin. She was Amy's mirror image, same blond hair and blue eyes, except Eloise stood four inches shorter, even in her cowboy boots. Amy always felt like a giraffe next to her cousin.

"I got up at three in the morning last Saturday," Amy said. "Packed five puppies and Jango in my car, and drove over an hour to pick you up when you decided to sneak out on your date after he fell asleep."

Eloise dropped the bag at Amy's feet. "We'll call it even."

Jango sniffed the food before looking up at them.

"Yes, that's for you, old man. Easier to digest," Amy said. "And better for you than puppy chow. You don't need the extra calories."

"But you do." Eloise held out a bag. "Blueberry muffin. I'm guessing you forgot to eat this morning."

"I was planning to grab a doughnut while I discussed the opening with the guys."

Eloise stepped around her and stood on her tiptoes to peer through the glass. "Wow. Talk about testosterone overload. I don't know how you do it. If I was in the same room with them, I wouldn't be able to form a coherent sentence. I'd be too busy trying to figure out which one would look best without his shirt."

Mark. Her brain heard the words *without his shirt*, and she thought of Mark. Those muscles begging to be touched, maybe more…

Amy swept her long bangs behind her ear, trying to erase the thought. Months had passed since she'd seen a half-naked Mark on her computer screen, and still, she couldn't forget the well-defined lines of his chest and his sculpted abs. Probably because he was the only half-naked man she'd seen in more than a year—the ones on the covers of her romance novels didn't count—but even if she wanted a hot fling, it wouldn't be with a man serving his country. Active-duty soldiers spelled heartbreak, and she'd learned that lesson already.

"My bet?" Eloise continued, gesturing to the men on

the other side of the window. "Gabe. But T.J.'s a close second."

"Stop," Amy said. "They're my brothers-in-law."

And Mark was like a pseudo-brother-in-law, too. Except she didn't think of him that way anymore. He was her friend, first, foremost and always. He was the one who had been there for her, talking to her each week, not only about Darren, but also about life. She spoke freely with him, holding almost nothing back. Almost. There were some things she couldn't share, especially not through a computer screen.

"Or maybe Luke," Eloise said. "The way that man talks about his dog, you can tell he loves her to pieces. It's so easy to trust a man who is crazy about his four-legged friend. And trust, well, that can be key in the bedroom. I bet—"

"Please, I'm begging you," Amy said. "I've known them forever."

"Doesn't change the fact that you are about to enter a room full of hotties. Maybe I should stick around and wait until you put them to work, so I can see those hard bodies in action."

"It's cold today. Even for March. I think they'll keep their clothes on while they work. And don't you have patients to see?"

Her cousin shrugged. "Two cats coming in for teeth cleanings. Both owners are young, single women. I'm sure they'd understand if I told them I had to watch the Benton brothers."

"Your feline patients might not be so understanding."

"True." Eloise moved away from the door. "I don't think they left you a doughnut. I didn't even see the box."

"I need to get in there. If I don't keep them busy, they'll get into trouble." Amy tossed the bag of dog food over her shoulder. "Thanks for driving out here. I couldn't handle a sick Jango on top of everything else."

"Anytime. If you need help keeping those boys busy, call me. I know a few ways to keep bachelor soldiers entertained."

"I'll keep that in mind," Amy said drily.

Eloise pointed at the bag. "And eat your muffin. You won the tall-gene lottery. You don't get to be super-skinny, too."

Amy waved to her cousin and went into her meeting, Jango following at her heels. "Hi, guys."

"Let me get that." Gabe, the oldest of the bunch, plucked the bag from her shoulder.

Her cousin had been right about one thing. The testosterone level in here was through the roof. Thank goodness the fourth brother, Jeremy, was still deployed. One more and she might have to take precautionary measures.

The Benton brothers each possessed an overwhelming male presence. When they got together, they were lethal. Three brown-haired, blue-eyed gods among men. And apart from T.J., the youngest and the runt at six feet, the brothers towered over mere five-foot-seven mortals like her.

Amy watched as Gabe placed the dog food bag on the ground, his biceps flexed. These men had to-die-for muscles. Eloise was right about that, too. Every woman in Heart's Landing would love to see these guys without their shirts.

Except Amy.

To her, the Benton brothers were walking, talking

reminders of the man she'd loved and lost. Darren had inherited the same blue eyes and brown hair. And like his brothers, Darren had walked into a room, and everyone had known he was there. They'd gravitated toward him. For most of their marriage, Amy had been by his side, content to bask in his glow.

But he was gone. The loss had been crushing at first. Darren had defined her world since she was fifteen. Year after year, she'd waited for him to come home and counted down the days until he deployed again. While he'd been on the other side of the world, she'd trained and boarded other people's pets, dreaming of the day when she would have her own kennel and raise her own dogs. But those plans had always taken a backseat to Darren's commitment to the SEALs.

Now, after eighteen months of mourning, she was ready to redefine her life.

"Do you want me to fill his bowl?" her brother-in-law asked, drawing her attention back to the office.

Amy shook her head. "I'll do it. He doesn't like it when others feed him."

Gabe stepped back. No one in this room would question Jango's preferences. Three of the four remaining Benton brothers were military war dog handlers, and T.J. worked as a vet at Lackland Air Force Base, caring for the animals and helping the trainers implement their programs.

"Great place, Ames," Luke said.

"Thanks," she said. All of Darren's family had started calling her Ames when Darren had first brought her around. They hadn't even been dating yet, but she'd already been part of the family. "How was your trip?"

"From Afghanistan?" Luke said. "Long, but uneventful. I'm looking forward to my two-week vacation before I report back."

"Well, this won't be a trip to the beach. I hope you got a good night's sleep and are ready to work today. I have a list of projects a mile long to get this place ready for the puppies. I would love to move them out of my spare bedroom before we officially open. Bullet, the father of this litter, has been living here for a while now, but I still have five puppies and their mama in the house."

T.J. clapped his hands together. "Bring it on."

"We want this place to be perfect. Mom said most of the town will be here for the opening reception and dedication," Luke added.

Amy nodded. Over the past few weeks, the simple ribbon-cutting ceremony for family and close friends had spiraled out of control. Amy had turned to her mother-in-law for help with the guest list, and the next thing she knew, one hundred and fifty people were coming to see her cut the ribbon. Caterers had been hired and a tent reserved. She was expected to give a speech.

"We're here, Ames," Gabe said. "For whatever you need."

"Good. You guys are my crew for the next few days. The tent arrives Thursday afternoon. I told the rental company that my volunteers could handle putting it together. I'm investing everything in the dogs and the reception."

Amy ran though her list of projects—build the obstacle course in the field, finish the fencing and install doggy doors so the pups could move between an indoor shelter and outdoor play area.

"Damn, Ames," T.J. said. "You've thought of everything. Your training course sounds better than Lackland's."

"These dogs will be the best," she said. Her pride would stand in the way of anything less. She understood what these dogs were capable of doing, and she knew the training they needed. When the DOD came to see them, her animals would be ready to ship out.

Gabe stepped forward and slung one arm over her shoulders, drawing her close to his side. "Darren would be so proud. He deserves this. To be remembered as a hero."

Darren had given his life for his country. That was the definition of the word, wasn't it? Whether she built a dog breeding facility in his honor would never change that fact. "He does," she said. "But—"

"But he always was your hero, wasn't he, Ames?" Gabe added. "Always perfect in your eyes."

No. Amy pressed her lips together, not saying a word. Darren had been her husband and her best friend. She would always love him. But there was a time, before his death, when he'd stopped being her hero.

Gabe shook his head. "How did my brother get so lucky? We were born and raised in the same town, went to the same high school, and not one of us found a girl like you."

"You found plenty of girls like me. I was under the impression you preferred to catch and release." She glanced at her audience, hoping for a laugh, or at least a smile.

Nothing.

Amy felt something heavy pressing against her leg and looked down to see Jango. Good boy, he'd sensed her tension and decided she needed him.

Amy crouched down. "Need to go out, buddy?"

The dog looked at her as if to say, *I can hold it, but you need to get out of here. Pronto.*

"I'll let you guys get started. I'll be up at the house with the dogs if you need anything." She stood and led Jango out the door.

"You got it, Amy. But don't worry about us. We'll have this place ready for you," Gabe said. "We'll swing by later after we pick up Mark and give you a progress report."

"Thanks." She followed Jango outside.

Four more days. She had to make it through the opening and dedication. After that, the Benton brothers would return to serving their country. She could pretend her dream was nothing more than a way to keep Darren's memory alive for a few days. For their sake. Maybe it would help them. Transforming her vision for this place into a reality had allowed her to restart her life after losing Darren. It had given her a reason to get out of bed each day.

But purpose infused the Benton brothers' lives. They served their country. For them, coming home was like opening an old wound. She had a hunch their grief felt fresh and overwhelming when they were back in Heart's Landing. They didn't see this town as a place to move forward. They came here to remember.

She stopped halfway between the farmhouse and the kennel, waiting while Jango marked a tree. Would Mark feel the same? Unease settled in her stomach, forming a tight ball.

For months now, their Sunday talks had centered on the present—how the kennel was progressing, her trip to Denmark to pick up the dogs she planned to breed and, when he felt like sharing, the lives he'd saved. Would coming home open old wounds? Would he join the others in the seemingly endless toast to her late husband's memory?

Probably. After all, Darren had been like a brother to Mark.

She crossed her arms in front of her chest, bracing against the cool March wind. Winter had lingered this year, refusing to give way to spring. Jango trotted back to her side, and they headed for the house to check on the puppies. It would be nice, she thought, hugging her arms tight, if someone saw how much she needed this place to be hers.

THREE HOURS LATER, Amy raced down the stairs in a T-shirt and underwear with Jango at her side.

"Let go," she called. Charlie and Foxtrot, the two most promising and troublesome puppies, ran in different directions, each holding a leg of her jeans between their teeth.

"Come on, guys, I need my pants," she said.

Foxtrot won the tug-of-war game, ripping the jeans from Charlie's mouth. Amy smiled. Out of this litter, Foxtrot showed the most promise. He had the drive to win. Just like a solider entering Basic Underwater Demolition/SEAL training had to want a place on the SEAL teams so badly he'd push past anything to get there, the dogs selected to work with the SEALs had to be the best. And being the best meant they never gave up. Every game of tug-of-war mattered. They had to win. Every ball thrown had to be retrieved. The dog wouldn't have it any other way. And that was Foxtrot, always the winner.

Charlie, the loser, tumbled but quickly recovered to chase his brother around the corner and into the kitchen.

Following them, she heard a loud rip. Maybe Charlie had it in him to serve with the SEALs, too. He'd just won half of her pants.

"Okay, you can keep the jeans," she said. "I'll find another pair. But I need you guys to go back to the guest room."

Ignoring her, the dogs disappeared from view, heading for the front room. While two stories, the farmhouse's footprint was small. A living room off the main entrance with a hall that led to the kitchen, the spare bedroom and the stairs. The upper floor featured an open, loft-style master bedroom. When the puppies escaped their room, they had free rein of the house. And she was starting to suspect they knew it. All the more reason to whelp this litter and move them into the kennel.

She heard a knocking from the front room followed by a series of barks and closed her eyes. She didn't want to know what they'd done to make that sound.

Amy rounded the corner and found the puppies on the couch shredding her jeans.

"Drop it," she said in a loud, authoritative tone.

This time they released her pants and looked up at her. But a second knocking diverted their attention. The front door.

"Amy?"

Oh, no. For the past eighteen months, she'd heard that voice through her computer every Sunday.

"Just a minute." But the puppies barked, drowning out her words. They jumped off the couch, taking her destroyed jeans with them.

She heard the knob turn, and Gabe say, "It should be unlocked. She knows we're coming."

Amy glanced down and groaned. Leopard-print undies with the words *Feeling Lucky* in big red letters. She'd bought them on sale months ago. At the time she'd thought no one would ever see them.

Her three brothers-in-law stepped into her living room. Mark followed, his rucksack over his shoulder, still wearing his uniform. She watched as four sets of eyes widened.

"Shit, Amy. The door was open. I'm sorry," Gabe said, redirecting his gaze. The rest of the brothers did the same, looking at the walls, the ceiling, anywhere but at her.

Not Mark. His were the only eyes in the room still fixed on her. And judging from the intensity of his stare, he wasn't embarrassed. He looked…interested. But it had been so long since a man had glanced at her with even a hint of desire that she was probably imagining it. She watched his lips move and realized he was reading the words on her underwear.

"The puppies stole my pants," she said.

Amy saw the exact moment it clicked for Mark. He heard her voice, and he no longer saw her as a woman in her undies, but as Darren's widow. That hint of desire, the one she may or may not have imagined, vanished. He looked away, shaking his head.

And great, now she was standing in a room full of drop-dead gorgeous men, in her underwear, and not one of them was looking at her.

3

FEELING LUCKY?

Mark read the red letters, knowing he should look away. The other guys radiated discomfort, shifting restlessly. But Mark couldn't do it.

Those long bare legs begged a man to fall to his knees and worship her. One glance and he knew he'd start by running his hands over her calves, gently guiding her legs farther apart, until he reached her thighs. He'd lean forward and run his lips, his tongue, his teeth over those red letters…

Shit, he shouldn't go there, not even in his freaking imagination. Make that *especially* not in his imagination after that dream he'd had on the flight back. But seeing Amy in her underwear uncovered a feeling that bordered on foreign. Desire, need, whatever the hell it was, looking at her, it hit him hard—and left him aching to touch and taste.

His gaze narrowed in, focusing on those sparkling words. If only luck was on his side.

While deployed, fear was his constant companion. It kept him vigilant, ready for the worst. The way he looked at it, skill kept him alive. Beneath the fear was a boatload of sadness and loss. Nothing lucky about that.

He heard her say something about puppies and pants. But Jango distracted him. One look at the dog and the desire vanished. The animal was like a shadow, always there. He was a four-legged, living and breathing reminder that Amy belonged to his best friend. He shouldn't be reading the words on her underwear. Not now, not ever.

"I'll go throw on some pants," she said. "Make yourselves at home."

Mark heard Amy's footsteps on the wooden floorboards, but kept his gaze trained on the wall. The stairs creaked, and he felt the brothers breathe a collective sigh of relief.

"Didn't need to see that," T.J. muttered.

"We should get back to work," Gabe said, turning to the door. "Tell Amy we'll catch up with her later. Over drinks at the Tall Pines Tavern?"

Mark nodded. "Sure thing. And thanks for the ride."

Luke slapped his shoulder as they walked past. "Anytime, man. Good to have you home."

The brothers hightailed it out the door. Mark dropped his rucksack on the floor and thought about following them. But it seemed like a bad idea to let the discomfort fester. Not when he'd come all this way to help her. He'd seen Amy in a bathing suit before. This wasn't any different.

Two puppies raced through the room, each dragging a piece of what he guessed had been her jeans. They paused to bark at him, the unfamiliar person in their home, and then raced off again with their prize.

Watching the remains of her pants disappear around

the corner, Mark realized a bathing suit was one thing. Leopard-print underwear was another. Someone was supposed to read those words—*feeling lucky*—and take action.

Was she seeing someone? She'd never said anything. But he was probably the last person she'd tell. Or at least on the list of last people. Darren's brothers were up there, too. If she was…well, hell, that was exactly what she needed. Someone new. A fresh start.

His jaw tightened. But whoever the guy was, he'd better be worthy of Amy. She'd been through so much. If some jerk thought he could breeze in and out of her life, Mark would be tempted to kick the shit out of him. And he had a feeling Darren's brothers would be next in line.

"Sorry about that." Amy walked into the room. This time she wore a pair of faded blue jeans and an oversize sweatshirt. She'd pulled her long hair into a ponytail. She looked exactly like the Amy he remembered from high school.

"They're six weeks old, and I've been doing some bite work with them," she said, speaking quickly, a sure sign she was still embarrassed. "Mostly chasing rags. They saw my jeans and thought it was a game."

Mark shrugged. "Most people are so excited to see me they forget their pants."

Funny or not, the joke worked its magic and diffused the discomfort.

Amy cocked her head to one side and smiled. "You save people. I guess that is to be expected."

She stepped closer, wrapping her arms around him, hugging him tight.

Mark closed his eyes. He couldn't recall the last time someone had held him. The flare of desire he'd sensed earlier was gone. Her hug? It was better than Thanksgiving dinner with all the fixings. It was pure comfort. Considering he'd been in Afghanistan less than forty-eight hours ago, it felt like a luxury.

"I missed you," she said. He felt her breath on his neck and moved away, breaking the physical connection before his body misinterpreted the way she was pressed up against him, and he started thinking about falling down on his knees and worshipping her again.

"Same here." The puppies raced around the corner, their paws sliding on the wooden floorboards. "Want some help rounding them up?"

"Let me grab some treats."

Mark followed her into the kitchen, taking in every detail. Nothing had changed. Pictures of Amy with her dogs, of her and Darren, hung on the walls. There was a large framed shot of her parents sitting on a boat.

"Your folks enjoying Florida?" he asked.

"They love it." She removed a handful of jerky treats from a jar. "My mom likes the weather, and she's thrilled to be closer to my grandmother. My aunt moved down there, too. They thought about coming west for the opening, but it's a long trip. I told them not to bother."

"That's too bad. What you're doing here is pretty impressive. I'm sure they'd be proud."

"Thanks, but you haven't even seen the kennels yet."

As if they'd smelled the treats through the walls, the puppies came running. Amy offered one to each dog as she led them around the corner. "Or met Nova and Bullet."

"The dogs you brought back from Europe?"

She nodded, opening the door to the spare bedroom. "I've been keeping Nova in here with her puppies while we finish the kennels. They should be able to move down in the next few days, before the opening. Until then, you're stuck on the couch. I hope that's okay."

"Long as I'm not in the way."

She knelt down beside a large Belgian Malinois and began rubbing her belly. "I'll be glad for the company."

He looked around the room. Two adult dogs, including Jango, and five puppies. "Looks like you have a full house already."

"I'd like to talk to someone who doesn't bark at me," she said. "Eloise doesn't count. The only time she stays here she is too drunk to drive home, or avoiding her latest romantic disaster."

"Sounds like the same old Eloise." He bent over and scooped up a tan puppy with a striking black nose and pointed ears. Mark was familiar with the breed, but also knew they were often mistaken for German shepherds. The little one in his hands bore a strong resemblance to the more popular breed.

"What about you?" Mark asked. "Are you seeing anyone?"

Amy froze, her hand on Nova's belly. "Wow, no one has asked me that."

Mark shrugged, turning the puppy onto her back. From a young age, war dogs were handled a lot, put in different positions to make them comfortable with anything. "Darren's been gone eighteen months."

"I know, but—I've been busy. Opening this place has taken all my time."

The tension Mark had been holding on to since he'd first thought her underwear might have an intended audience slipped away.

"And I haven't exactly been looking," she added.

"Then your couch sounds great. An upgrade from the crowded barracks."

Amy stood and turned to him. He knew that look. She'd worn the same expression when she won homecoming queen. Pure astonishment.

"You thought you'd be in the way because I was seeing someone?" She let out a laugh.

"Yeah," he said, looking up at her. "It's not such a crazy idea."

He cut himself off before he said things he couldn't take back. Amy didn't need to know that he'd taken one look at her bare legs and thought about running his hands up her limbs because, shit, his mind should never have traveled down that road. She might be single, but that didn't mean he was the guy to fill the empty space in her bed.

"Sometimes it still kind of feels like it is," she said softly. Then she gave a little shake of her head and turned to the door. "You came all this way, I think I owe you a tour."

"Love one." He returned the puppy to his mother and held the door for Amy and Jango.

With the sun sinking low in the sky, they walked through the yard to the kennel. It was double in size, compared to the previous structure. He knew she'd done well with her dog training and boarding business, and enjoyed it, but a building this size suggested she was seriously committed to her new venture.

He stopped a few feet from the door, resting his hands on his hips as he studied the new kennel. She'd painted it white with a forest green trim. It looked shiny and new.

"Impressive," he said.

She looped her arm through his. “You haven’t seen the inside yet.”

He followed her through the reception area into a long hall with individual rooms lining either side. Peering through an open door, he saw that each room held a doghouse and two doors—one doggy and one human—to a small fenced outdoor area.

“I tried to replicate the kennels where the SEAL teams kept their dogs,” she said. “On a smaller scale, of course.”

“You did a kick-ass job.” The place was amazing. How she’d pulled it together in only a few months, while working to secure the funds from the bank, astonished him.

“When Darren was home, I would ask him to draw sketches of the kennels Jango lived in. He also made lists of changes he wanted to make and things he’d keep the same. And I added some of my own ideas, too.”

Mark paused and leaned against the entry to a modern, brand-new veterinary exam room.

“You should be proud of yourself.”

Her lips curved, offering a hint of a smile. “I am.”

“Are you planning to head out with the guys tonight?” He stepped into the exam room, closer to her. After seeing her in her underwear, he knew he should keep his distance. But he couldn’t do it. “To Tall Pines Tavern?”

“I might drop by. I think the puppies are old enough now to be left alone for an hour or two. Maybe I’ll see if Mrs. Benton can stop in and check on them.”

“How about I take you to dinner first?” he said, running his hand over the metal table’s smooth surface. “Toast your success.”

Amy blinked. Shit, he’d surprised her. Too late to

take it back now. He kept his gaze fixed on her, but out of the corner of his eye, he saw Jango stand. The animal looked ready to attack. It was as if he'd understood Mark's words but misinterpreted his intentions. This was just dinner between two friends. And that was all they'd ever be—friends.

AMY STARED AT MARK as if he was speaking a foreign language. She'd eaten dinner with Mark hundreds of times. But there was something about this invitation that sent her mind spiraling back to the flash of longing she'd seen in his eyes earlier. The thought of sitting across from him, sharing a meal, his attention focused on her…

"I…um…yes. Okay," she said, feeling like a giddy schoolgirl.

He nodded. "Is Lucia's Italian place still open?"

"It is. But I think they changed their sauce. It's too sweet now. There's a new Mexican place in town that makes the best enchiladas."

"Your night, your choice."

"Mexican it is." Amy led Mark back into the kennel's central hall. "But I need to finish up a few things first. Check with the guys. I'll come find you in an hour."

Mark nodded. "Sounds like a plan."

He headed for the exit, his hands shoved in his pockets. She had a lot to do before dinner, but she didn't move until the door closed behind him. It felt good, seeing him in the flesh instead of on a screen. And the fact that he, of all people, understood what she was trying to do here—that meant so much.

Amy turned and moved toward the sound of hammers pounding, planning to tell the Benton brothers to call it quits for the day But she stopped out of sight of where the brothers were working and closed her eyes. She felt Jango sit by her side and press up against her leg. Reaching down, she touched the dog's head.

Part of her still felt married and that even the smallest hint of desire was a betrayal. But Darren was gone. And eighteen months was a long time. Moving forward—she was allowed to want that, wasn't she?

"I've waited," she whispered. "For so long."

In high school, she'd waited for Darren to notice her. After that she'd waited for him to ask her out and, later, marry her. Then she'd waited three hundred days out of every year for him to come home.

She'd put her dream business on hold because Darren wasn't ready to quit his SEAL team. After his death, she'd waited for the grief to fade, knowing only time would help her heal. And it had. But now, after spending the past twelve years in a holding pattern, she was done waiting.

Jango turned his head up, licking the palm of her hand. "Even if I am ready to put myself out there and start dating, Mark isn't the guy," she whispered.

Yes, he was gorgeous—especially with his shirt off. But that didn't change the fact that he'd been her husband's best friend.

4

FOR THE FIRST TIME in months, Amy felt full. Enchiladas, chips, guacamole—she'd devoured all of it while discussing her plans for the kennel. Mark sat opposite her, listening and occasionally surveying the restaurant.

Amy studied the collar of his button-down shirt peeking out from underneath his sweater. When had he started wearing dress shirts? He'd always been a T-shirt kind of guy. Maybe a sweatshirt or flannel in the colder months. Nothing that drew attention. And in Heart's Landing a button-down in a place where no one dressed for dinner was bound to make people look twice. She'd already caught half a dozen diners, mostly women, glancing their way.

Or maybe it had nothing to do with his shirt. At six-four, Mark towered over most men. A sweater and dress shirt didn't exactly hide his broad chest and powerful arms. Of course, she'd seen those muscles stripped bare…

She pushed the thought away and tried to focus on the here and now.

"You look nice." She waved at his collar. "Fancy shirt."

Mark shrugged. "I travel light, especially when I know I won't be back long. And I wanted to look decent for your opening."

Back, not *home*. Didn't he still consider Heart's Landing home? If not here, where? His words sank in further. He was leaving again soon. She'd known that from day one. Mark had a month's leave at most, and he hadn't said how much of that time he planned to spend in Oregon. But still, hearing him say it thrust her into the past. She'd hated the goodbyes, could still feel the dread.

"You could wear your dress uniform," she said, scraping the last of the guacamole from the bowl even though her appetite had vanished.

"I will if you'd prefer. But I figured you already had Gabe walking around in his navy whites. Plus Luke and T.J. in their dress uniforms."

And Mark had always been more comfortable in the background. In high school, he'd been a star on the football team—and an attractive one with his wavy brown hair and rich brown eyes. He'd drawn half the cheerleading squad's attention. Yet, he'd always hung back.

"Wear whatever you're comfortable in. I'm just glad you're here." She polished off her last chip and pushed the bowl away.

"You were hungry. We could always order another."

"I can't eat another bite. But if you want more, go ahead."

Mark shook his head, his eyes darting to the door and back. She wanted to reassure him that nothing bad was likely to happen in their quiet little town. But she suspected he already knew that.

"How does it feel to be here?" she asked gently. "The transition from Afghanistan to a sleepy town in the middle of nowhere has to be a culture shock."

"Like I've walked into the past," he said grimly.

"Not much changes here," she acknowledged. "Mrs. Marlowe is still running the general store. And half of the people in town head over to Tall Pines to drink and dance every night. Not that I go much, but Eloise drags me in every so often. Most people haven't changed since high school, just aged a bit, gotten married and had babies."

She was rambling on and on, but she wanted to lighten the mood. If Mark needed to talk, of course she'd listen. He'd been there for her in the early months, first in person and later through the computer screen. But she'd rather close the door to heavy conversation, at least for one night.

Mark smiled. "I think you've thrown Heart's Landing a curveball with your kennel."

And just like that, the door slammed shut. "Everyone in town…they've been very supportive."

"Your passion for those dogs is contagious. They feel that and want to be a part of what you're doing."

Amy cocked her head, studying him. "You really mean that, don't you?"

"That you're a passionate woman? Yes."

Amy laughed. That comment was pure Mark. If she hadn't known him since elementary school, she would have thought he was flirting with her.

"Wow, that came out wrong." He ran his hands through his short brown hair. The waves all the girls had admired in high school had been lost to a military buzz cut.

"I guess some things don't change," she said. "You still have a way with words."

"Yeah, being here makes me feel like I'm back in high school. Opening my mouth and sticking my foot in."

"Like when you picked Molly McAdams up for a first date and you promised her father that you wouldn't do any of the things you wanted to do with her?"

"Her dad came to the door with a shotgun. I was trying to tell him I wouldn't lay a hand on his daughter. It came out wrong."

"Molly thought it was hysterical. She told everyone the next day."

"I remember," he said. "I learned to keep my mouth shut and avoid girls whose fathers owned guns."

Amy laughed. "That was everyone in school."

"I know."

Amy paged through her memory. Mark had steered clear of other girls after Molly. Maybe that incident, and the way Molly had retold the story of Mark's fumbled words for the rest of their junior year, had bothered him more than he'd let on.

Staring across the table at the tall, muscular man, she didn't see the quiet boy she remembered from high school. Yes, he'd just given her a verbal reminder, but the man who'd said the wrong thing was not the same person she video chatted with each week.

"You're different when you're deployed," she said. "More focused and intense."

Any trace of humor faded away. "I have to be. I lead a team of men. When a mission drops, we can't mess around. I need my team to follow my orders."

Amy nodded. Lives depended on him. Just thinking about it was sobering.

"Mark, how did you know that you wanted to be a PJ?" she asked. "You could have stayed here and become a doctor if you wanted to save lives."

"Medical school was a little out of my reach."

In high school, she'd asked Darren if Mark's mom minded that her son ate dinner with the Benton family six out of seven nights a week. *She's not home,* Darren had said. *If he wasn't here, Mark would be alone. And I don't think there is much to eat at his place.*

"I think we both know how much the people over there need help," he added. "Getting soldiers home to their loved ones, that's what I'm good at."

"It's your passion."

"It's a job, Amy. Just a job."

She reached across the table and placed her hand over his. "I wouldn't be so sure about that."

He tensed as if the touch surprised him, but didn't pull away. Turning his hand over, he interlaced his fingers with hers, holding tight. A taut energy radiated from his touch. And she didn't want to let go. She felt his strong presence through the computer each week. But this—this was more.

Or maybe she was imagining things. Maybe dormant desire had chosen this moment to rise to the surface, demanding she pay attention.

His gaze met hers across the table, searching and intent. It was as if he was trying to decode the meaning behind her words and the way her hand held his.

I want—

Mark's phone vibrated on the table, silencing the errant thoughts. He picked it up, scanning the screen. "It's Luke. They're at Tall Pines. We've been ordered to join them."

"We can't avoid your welcome home forever." She smiled. "I'll get the check. Are you okay to split it?"

"I'm buying, Amy. I insist."

The way he said those words left her nodding. "Okay, but your first drink at the bar is on me."

"Deal." Mark signaled to the waitress.

After settling up, they headed for the door. Part of her wished they could stay here, just the two of them, joking about the past and learning more about the people they'd become. But it was only a matter of time before the Benton brothers would come looking for them, determined to drag them both into the town spotlight.

MARK HESITATED, HIS HAND on the door to the tavern. He could hear the live country band and the stomp of cowboy boots on the dance floor from the street. The place would be packed. Not many bars around here and with the Benton brothers in town everyone would be at Tall Pines tonight.

He glanced over at Amy. Mark wanted to return to the quiet intimacy of the restaurant and keep her to himself for a little longer. Coming home, he felt as if he'd pulled on boots that he'd outgrown years ago. But with Amy he could kick them off and relax. Right now, that sounded a helluva lot better than facing old friends from school.

"Ready?" she asked, moving to his side.

"It's crowded in there."

She bit her lip, and he felt her shifting away as if she might turn around and head back to her truck. "I had a bad feeling it would be," she said. "The guys likely rounded everyone up. Told them you were home."

"We can leave. I'll text Luke, tell him you're tired and that I had to drive you home."

"No. It's your first night back. You should have fun. Drink. Visit with friends. I'll be fine." She glanced through the window beside the door. "As long as I stay off the dance floor."

Mark frowned. "You were always the first one out there. To this day, you're still the only person who has ever made me dance."

"And your junior prom date loved that."

"She knew it was part of the deal in advance," he said. "But you stayed on the floor until they kicked us out of the gym."

"I'm not up for dancing tonight. Too much Mexican food," she said, glancing at the window again. "Mind if I hold on to your arm?"

His brow furrowed. "Sure."

She stepped closer, looping her arm through his, leaning into him. Shock waves pulsed through him as if her body touching his set off a chain reaction heading south. And he sure as shit was going to stop it before that happened.

Mark told himself it was a matter of getting readjusted to living in a world that wasn't peopled with his teammates and injured soldiers, where touch was more than a dying man's hand in his and a fellow PJ slapping him on the back. His reaction had nothing to do with Amy's slim legs or soft curves.

"If I tell them I twisted my ankle I won't have to dance," she said. "You know, if anyone asks. And they always do when I come here."

Mark frowned. "You're serious about not dating."

"That, too."

He stared at the Tall Pines's wooden door. "It's been more than a year, Amy."

"I know, but..."

She started to move away, and he refused to let her go. Placing his hand on her arm, he kept her close. "But what?" he demanded. "What's holding you back?"

"When I start dating again," she said softly, "I need to find someone who sees me."

"Okay, I get that," he said, glancing down at her. Was he like the others? When he looked at Amy, what did he see?

A slim blond-haired, blue-eyed beauty with long legs—shit, a man would have to be half-dead not to fantasize about running his hands up her limbs. But looking down at her, Mark couldn't set aside the fact that Amy was so much more than a beautiful blonde. He saw a woman who was working her tail off to establish her new business breeding dogs to help soldiers and law enforcement in the field.

"It's a big step," he said. "You deserve someone who respects you. You should take as much time as you need."

"Thanks." She let out a sigh. "But on the flip side, I miss dating. I miss sex. After all, I am a 'passionate woman.'"

"Not going to live that one down for a while, am I?" he said, doing his best to separate the words *Amy* and *sex* in his head.

"Nope. Not for a while." Her smile faded as she glanced through the window at the crowded dance floor. "So, are you willing to play along and pretend I stumbled getting down from the truck?"

"As long as I get to keep you company in the non-dancing section," he said.

"Deal."

Mark opened the door and stepped inside. The smell of stale beer hit him, bringing back memories. There had been a time in his teens when walking into this place and inhaling that scent had seemed like a dream. He'd sneaked in once with some of the guys from the football team, but they'd been kicked to the curb the minute they'd tried to order a drink. The bartender had threatened to call their mamas if they came back before their twenty-first birthdays.

Looking at the place now, not much had changed. A wooden bar ran down one side of the restaurant, lined with stools. The cramped stage stood on the opposite side. A live country band, probably local, played fast and furious, strumming guitars and fiddles, pounding away at the drum kit, while the crowd danced. Wooden tables and mismatched chairs filled the space between the bar and the dance floor.

He spotted the Benton brothers standing by a table, holding court. Some of the men and women were familiar, old friends from school, and some were new. T.J. saw them first and waved. Mark headed over, taking it slow as Amy leaned against him.

Her hand held tight to his forearm, and even through the fabric of his clothes, her touch bordered on intimate. Mark's jaw tightened as he mentally swept that thought away alongside Amy and sex. But with Amy's slim figure aligned with his, from where her shoulder pressed up against his biceps down to where her hip touched his thigh, it was easy to buy into her little white lie. To pretend that she needed him, holding her, supporting her, and… Shit, what he needed was a drink.

"Oh, Eloise," Amy murmured. Mark followed her gaze. Amy's cousin was standing close to Gabe's side.

And the eldest Benton brother wasn't fighting her off. Just the opposite. He had his hand on her lower back, holding her close. Mark doubted Eloise had sprained her ankle, too.

Mark and Amy reached the table as Luke raised his glass. "About time you joined us. We've been toasting your homecoming without you."

Completing the semicircle of brothers, T.J. stood beside Luke, studying the nonexistent space between Mark's body and Amy. "Something wrong, Ames?"

She tensed at the nickname, her fingers digging into his arm. "Twisted my ankle in the parking lot."

T.J. stepped forward. "Want me to take a look at it?"

"You're a vet, not a medic," Mark said, leading a limping Amy to one of the two empty chairs.

"I didn't realize they were calling the PJs out for twisted ankles," T.J. shot back.

"I've got her." Mark lowered Amy down, his hands on her arms and his face close to hers.

"You don't have to put on a show," she whispered.

"I don't mind." It beat handing her off to one of the cowboys hovering nearby ready and willing to swing her onto the dance floor. He'd counted three men looking her way as they'd hobbled toward the Benton brothers. Despite what Amy might believe, those men hadn't seen her long, jean-clad legs or her wide blue eyes and thought widow. He'd bet money there wasn't an ounce of pity in any one of them.

Mark lower himself onto one knee beside Amy's feet and lifted her calf up, resting it across his thigh. "Let's have a look."

He slipped her shoe off, running his hands up to her ankle. He'd spent the past few months treating strangers, but touching them had never felt personal. With Amy, it was. Her skin was soft and smooth. The ruby-red nail polish on her toes caught the bar's dim lighting, pulling his focus from his job.

Mark held Amy's foot in one hand, turning it left and right, while his other hand rested on her calf, drifting higher than necessary. "Does this hurt?"

Amy nodded. "It does. When you turn it to the side. But just a bit."

His fingers traced the curve of her ankle, his touch bordering on teasing. If anyone looked too closely, they'd realize Mark had stretched the definition of "ankle exam." He looked up at her, hoping like hell she couldn't see the heat he felt pulsing through his body in his gaze.

"Good news," he said.

"I'll live?" Her eyes sparkled with mischief.

He nodded. "It's not sprained. Rest it for a bit, and you'll be back on your feet by the end of the night."

"But no dancing?" she asked as he slipped her shoe back on and lowered her foot to the floor.

"I wouldn't recommend it." Mark stood. "I'll get you a drink. What are you having?"

"White wine, please." He could hear the hint of laughter in her tone, as if she'd enjoyed their little performance. "But I'm buying, remember?"

"You can pay me back later," he said before she reached for her purse. "I don't want you to disturb your ankle. Save me a seat?"

Amy patted the empty chair beside. "All yours."

He placed their order at the bar and turned to watch the dance floor. He knew most of these people, and even the ones he didn't looked like locals. Not many tourists in Heart's Landing. Sure, they were close to the coast, but most visitors preferred the towns on the water.

The music switched from upbeat to slow and romantic. Couples moved closer or left the floor. Out of the corner of his eye, he spotted two familiar faces and frowned. Gabe and Eloise had abandoned the group table in favor of the dance floor, pressing up close to each other.

Mark shook his head as he paid for the drinks. He hoped they knew what they were doing. The ties between the two families ran deep. A one-night stand could lead to hurt feelings and broken friendships. If not tomorrow, then when Gabe returned to his team. But maybe they'd found a way to avoid all that emotional crap and just have a good time. Hell, maybe he should ask for a road map.

5

AMY STARED AT the dance floor. She should be out there. Dancing. Laughing. Flirting. It didn't matter if half the men in the bar looked at her and thought, *There goes Darren's widow.* That wasn't how she saw herself. Not anymore. And it was time to do something about it. Before her body's reaction to a pretend ankle exam ruined her relationship with one of her closest and oldest friends.

Mark had touched her in a crowded bar, and she'd been tempted to press her bare foot against his thigh. The moment had felt intimate and wild. But she suspected that was only partly due to the way his hands had moved over her skin—and partly due to their shared secret. She kept so many locked away that having a partner in this ruse sent misguided signals to parts of her body she'd ignored for a year and a half.

She stole a look at Mark, standing at the bar. He was like a guard dog, keeping watch over her as he waited for her wine. He offered so much more than a shared confidence, she realized. If she stumbled, Mark would catch her. Always. He was her safety net, her friend, and damn it, she couldn't stop thinking about the look in his eyes when he'd seen her in her underwear. Hunger?

"Hey, Ames." T.J. sat down in the chair next to hers, holding a beer bottle in one hand. "If you need crutches, I think we have some at the house from when Luke busted his knee. I could head back and pick them up for you."

Amy smiled, patting his arm. "Thanks, but that won't be necessary. I'll be back on my feet soon."

"I can help with the dogs in the morning," T.J. added.

"I'm going to take you up on that offer, but not because I'm injured," she said, welcoming the distraction from her wayward thoughts of Mark. "I need your advice on how to introduce new scents to the puppies. I was thinking about using rags soaked in the different chemicals they will be expected to detect."

"That's a good plan," T.J. said, leaning forward in his chair, wrapping both hands around his beer bottle. "The most important thing is to keep the materials free and clear of your scent. Wear rubber gloves when you're handling the rags."

Mark returned and handed her a wineglass. She sipped slowly, trying to take mental notes as T.J. talked. But with Mark sitting close by, her focus splintered. She drew a deep breath, inhaling his familiar masculine smell. Sandalwood, possibly from his aftershave. If she leaned closer, pressing her nose, maybe her lips, to his jaw, tracing the contours as she licked, kissed and breathed him in, then she'd know for certain.

Amy shifted in her chair, nodding to T.J., though she hadn't heard what he'd said. Her imagination was spiraling out of control. A fake ankle exam didn't lead to kisses. But there was something about the way he'd touched her—

"Mark!" The loud, shrill call silenced Amy's internal monologue. She watched as Molly McAdams strutted across the bar, doing her best imitation of a runway walk in her high heels and fitted skirt.

"You're home!" Molly added.

With the faintest hint of a smile, Mark rose from his chair, allowing Molly to wrap her arms around him, pressing her breasts against his chest.

"Hey there, Molly," he said.

Molly drew back just enough to look up at Mark's face as she swept her long, straight black hair over her shoulder with one hand. The fingers on her right hand held tight to Mark's biceps.

Amy frowned. She had nothing against Molly. They'd never been friends, but Amy always said hello in the grocery store. Still, did Molly have to stand so close to Mark?

"How about a dance?" Molly flashed a wide smile.

"No, thanks." He glanced down at her. "Promised I'd keep Amy company."

Molly laughed. "I think T.J. is up for the task."

"Maybe. But I'm still recovering from the long trip home and need to save my energy to help her out tomorrow." Mark rocked back on his heels, trying to extricate himself from Molly's arms.

"A rain check, then." Molly arched slightly, offering Mark a peek down the front of her low-cut fitted tank. "Don't be a stranger, Mark. I'm still living on the family farm. And you don't have to worry about Daddy. We moved him to an assisted-living condo last year and took away his guns. He's at the retirement community, where I've been working for the past few years as the programming director."

"That's great, but—"

Molly leaned closer but didn't bother dropping her voice. "I have the whole house to myself now. My brother moved to San Francisco. Plenty of room to do all those things you wanted to do in high school. We can make as much noise as you want."

Amy supposed it was wrong to dislike a woman who spent her days planning activities for seniors. But after hearing Molly's not-so-subtle invitation, it was hard to feel charitable toward her.

"We should save him," she muttered.

"Mark? He can take care of himself," T.J. said. "And I'm not so sure he wants to walk away. Hell, I wouldn't."

"T.J.," she said, turning to her brother-in-law. "You can't be serious."

He shrugged. "I wouldn't turn down a chance to make some noise with her."

Amy blinked and glanced back at Mark. He'd leaned in close to Molly, dropping his voice too low for Amy to overhear his words. But she didn't miss the color in his cheeks as he stepped back, breaking free from Molly's hold.

T.J. stood and headed for the bar, offering to buy Amy a second drink, but she declined. More alcohol would not help. It might make the unwelcome spark of jealousy worse. She did not have a claim to Mark, and she never would. But still, seeing him with Molly…

A second later, Mark sank into T.J.'s chair and reclaimed his beer. Amy watched and waited, but he didn't say a word.

"One of the guys can help me home," she said. "If you're heading out."

Mark raised an eyebrow. "To do all the things I wanted to do in high school?"

She nodded, jealousy bubbling up inside.

He held his beer bottle up to his lips as the band started a familiar country line dance. Out of the corner of her eye, Amy saw T.J. join a woman she didn't recognize at the bar.

"High school is not a time in my life I'm interested in revisiting," Mark said, lowering his drink. "I'm planning to help you home and crash on your couch if that's all right with you."

"Yes, but—"

Mark's hand covered hers. "I'm not interested in starting something."

With Molly? Or with anyone?

Mark withdrew his hand, turning his attention back to the dance floor. "Though I have to admit, I was surprised at how much she has changed."

Amy followed Molly's movements on the dance floor. "Implants. I'm surprised you didn't notice last time you visited. She's had them for a few years. Drew a lot of attention when she first got them."

"Bet her daddy loved that," Mark said, shaking his head.

"She took away his guns soon after." Amy shifted in her chair, flexing her foot.

"How's the ankle?" he asked.

"I'm fine, Mark."

He chuckled. "I know. Are you sure you wouldn't rather be dancing?"

"Is that an invitation?" She looked out at the crowded

floor, scanning the familiar faces for Gabe and her crazy cousin. She'd spotted them dancing in the corner minutes ago.

"Nope. But when T.J. gets back with his beer, I'm sure he'd be willing."

"Thanks, but—" Amy frowned, leaning forward in her chair. "I don't see them."

"Who?"

"Eloise and Gabe. They're not on the dance floor anymore. They've been glued to each other all night."

"Your cousin is a big girl. She can take care of herself."

Amy shook her head. "I don't know. Gabe might be too much, even for her."

MARK SIGHED AS he scanned the bar. He'd rather sit here teasing Amy—perhaps get to the bottom of why she'd looked as if she wanted to tear Molly McAdams apart—than start a search party for Eloise and Gabe.

Still, Amy had a point. All the Benton brothers served. But Gabe, like Darren, had joined the SEALs. He'd never been on the same team as his brother, but Gabe possessed the same draw. Hero. Larger than life. The fact that he was a war dog handler tended to make women fall at his feet. And Mark knew Gabe was usually more than willing to pick them up—for a night or two.

What if Eloise, the country vet and unabashed animal lover, hadn't thought this through?

Mark set his beer down on the table. "Want to find them?"

"No." Amy looked down at her foot, resting on a chair. "My ankle. I can't magically heal it."

"I could give you a piggyback ride." He'd had one thought when Molly had pressed up against him—escape. But the idea of Amy's limbs wrapped around him pushed him in the opposite direction.

"Hard to execute a covert search and rescue that way," she said drily.

"I doubt Eloise is in danger," he said. "Gabe's a good guy."

"You're right. Of course they're fine." She pulled out her cell as T.J. rejoined the table. "But I should go outside and check on the puppies. No service in here."

"Mom's got them," T.J. said, resting a hand on her shoulder. "Relax, Ames."

He wasn't sure if it was the nickname or the way T.J. touched her, but Mark stood, pulling Amy up with him. "Lean on me. I'll help you to the front."

Like competitors in a three-legged race, they hobbled away from the table. Mark pushed open the door, keeping Amy close. Out here, it was probably safe to drop the ankle ruse, but she didn't let go. And he didn't feel like pushing her away.

But Amy stopped at the edge of the parking lot and released his arm. Standing on her own two feet again, she dialed and lifted the phone to her ear. Mark followed as she walked out into the lot. He overheard her leave a quick message, saying she'd be back soon.

Slipping her cell into her pocket, she turned to him. "I should probably head home. If you want to stay, I'm sure one of the guys would give you a ride."

"I'll go with you."

They headed for her truck, weaving between the parked cars. Mark scanned the area out of habit and stilled when he saw a truck labeled Eloise Jones Veterinary Care, in the corner of the lot. In the front seat was Eloise, looking as if she was riding her very own SEAL. And that sight was a lot more surprising than Molly McAdams's fake breasts.

One glimpse told him Eloise wasn't calling the shots. She had her arms bound behind her back with what looked like her bra. Her eyes were closed and her head was thrown back as she moved and arched over a fully dressed Gabe. Or maybe he'd stripped off his pants. Mark couldn't tell from here, and he wasn't about to take a closer look. He'd already seen too much.

"What?" Amy said, stopping beside him.

"Nothing," he said shaking his head, trying to steer her away. But it was too late. She'd already spotted Eloise's truck.

"Oh," she said. "Wow."

He watched her eyes widen, saw the moment her breath caught. Her cheeks flushed, and he saw shock, embarrassment and what looked an awful lot like longing in her eyes…

Mark ground his teeth together, pushing hard against the simmering feelings building up, demanding that he reach for her, offer an answer to the desire written on her face. But he couldn't. He couldn't *want* Amy. There were some lines he wouldn't cross, and sleeping with his best friend's widow was one of them. But that line was becoming more indistinct by the moment, and he needed to stay a few feet away from the barrier, not inch closer to it. Yes, he believed Amy should move on with her life. But not with him. She deserved so much more.

He took her arm and led her away. Seeing Eloise and Gabe—it was all kinds of wrong. It was erotic and hot, but not a moment that needed witnesses.

"I guess I didn't need to worry about her," Amy said with a laugh. "Looks like she has the situation under control."

Someone had control in that truck, but Mark wasn't sure it was Eloise. "They could have waited until they got home," he said tightly.

"There's something to be said for claiming the moment. Sometimes I wish I could be that free," she murmured. "It looks like a lot more fun than my vibrator."

The spark of the need he'd felt while watching Amy's reaction flared. The image of Amy with her arms bound, waiting for him to touch her, taste her... Shit, he'd even use her vibrator, teasing her with the toy until she begged for more. For him.

Mark clenched his jaw, pushing the images away. Picking up the pace, he led her to the truck.

"We need to go," he said, his words clipped and his tone rough. *"Now."*

FIVE MINUTES LATER, Mark stared straight ahead at the dark country road. Tonight had verged off course. It felt as if they were scrambling to make a U-turn and go back to where they'd started the evening.

The thought of Amy wanting to be free, to live in the moment... Mark shifted his hips trying to get comfortable, but with an erection that left him feeling like a seventeen-year-old kid again, it just wasn't possible. Probably because the reason he was turned on wasn't back in the Tall Pines parking lot, but sitting beside him in the truck. He'd been focused on one thing—getting out of there—until Amy had started talking about living in the moment and her damn sex toys.

Drawing a deep breath, Mark mentally ran through his checklist for stocking his helicopter.

"I'm sorry," Amy said.

"For what?" Mark kept his gaze fixed on the road. "When you suggested we look for Eloise and Gabe, I have a feeling you didn't think we'd find them like that."

"I'm not apologizing for my cousin. If you need an apology, you can take that up with her or Gabe."

"Not going to happen."

"I'm sorry for making you uncomfortable," she said. "For talking to you as if you were one of my girlfriends. You don't need to know about me and my, well…I'll stop talking now."

"You can tell me anything, Amy," Mark said quietly. "You don't have to hold back on my account."

"Okay."

Mark heard the uncertainty in her voice. He hated the fact that she'd raised her guard around him. "What you said earlier about being free?"

She nodded.

"You can be." He reached for the stick, shifting gears. "I'm not saying you should do it in a bar parking lot—"

"I wouldn't," she said. "I'm not that wild. I want… Oh, God, sometimes the need to feel and be with someone is just so strong. But the thought of dating, of finding someone, it scares me. I should probably just do it and get past that first time. Maybe in another town. A quick one-night stand with someone removed from Heart's Landing."

No. Swerving to the shoulder of the two-lane highway, Mark fought the urge to fill the cab of the truck with that one word.

"Mark?" Amy said, her eyes widening as he put the truck in Park.

"Look at me, Amy," he demanded. She obeyed, and he saw the question in her blue eyes. What was he doing? Hell if he knew. But he was damn certain he wasn't going to let her leap into bed with a stranger.

"I want you to promise me one thing. You won't run off and settle for a quickie with some stranger. You should have a man who gives you what you want. But no more hiding. No more sprained ankles or talking about picking up a random guy. Find someone who can give you what you need. Someone you can trust."

She raised an eyebrow. "Volunteering?"

The thought of fulfilling her needs, making her scream his name… Mark ground his teeth. What he wanted didn't matter. He wasn't the man for her. He did fun and temporary. Nothing more. "No."

"Why not?" she challenged, leaning closer.

The need to touch her overrode rational thought. He raised one hand, running his finger over the exposed skin above the neckline of her shirt. "I don't do relationships."

"I'm not asking for one."

His finger dipped below the fabric of her shirt, running over the swell of her breast. He wanted to say yes, draw her onto his lap right here, right now, and drive her wild. But he couldn't.

He withdrew his hand. "Amelia Mae, I would never forgive myself if I damaged our friendship."

"You won't." She reached for him, her palm cupping the side of his face. Sweet and gentle. Christ, between the things he wanted from her and the big pile of nothing he had to offer in return, he had to say no.

He caught her wrist, lowering her hand to her lap. "Yeah, I would. Because one night with you… Hell, I know it wouldn't be enough. For either of us."

6

"I WANT TO FEEL you move." His voice was low and rough. With one finger, he stroked the length of her neck. "Beneath me, on top of me."

Oh, God, she wanted that, too. Every inch of her body begged for it. She stepped forward, but he caught her before she could run her hands over his muscles—the ones she'd admired and longed to touch.

He put his hands on her shoulders and held her in place. "I need to know you want this, too. I need to hear you say the words, Amelia Mae."

"I want this," she whispered. "I want you."

His hands moved over her shoulders to her bare arms. Thank goodness for sleeveless shirts. She arched her back, craving more. He reached her wrists and paused, wrapping his hands around them and holding her tight. She closed her eyes, excitement pulsing through her.

"Say my name," he demanded.

"I want you, Mark. Just you."

Somewhere, deep inside, her subconscious screamed,

This is Mark! *And panic rose. What was she doing here? She needed to leave, to break free and walk away...*

His lips touched her neck, trailing kisses up to her ear, and she closed her eyes.

No, she couldn't leave. It had been so long since anyone had touched her, kissed her.

He released her wrists, but didn't let her go. Holding her hips, he ran one hand up the side of her body, stopping before he reached her bra line. His palm moved around to the front, teasing and taunting, but never touching her breasts as he shifted to her stomach, teasing the top of her drawstring pants. His fingers dipped below the elastic band, and her breath caught. As if he sensed her anticipation building and swirling, he stopped, his fingertips running along the top of her underwear.

"Are you feeling lucky, Amelia Mae?"

She nodded.

"Good." His index finger traced small circles over her lower belly. "Spread your legs for me. Let me in."

She obeyed, moving her feet apart. And he rewarded her, the circles moving lower until they brushed back and forth over the one place that could make her scream.

"I've wanted to touch you like this for so damn long," he murmured. "I've fought it, but seeing you again... I can't fight it anymore. I need to feel you, wet and ready for me. I want you out of your mind with pleasure, screaming and calling out my name as you come. First like this, with my hands on you. And then when I'm inside you."

His fingers moved lower, one slipping inside as the heel of his hand pressed down against her, driving her closer and closer. But something was holding her back, preventing her from falling headfirst into a mind-numbing orgasm.

"Mark, please more!"

Amy opened her eyes, the sound of her words echoing in the empty room. Her fingers clutched the sheets. Her body shifted restlessly, craving release. But unless she replaced Mark's imaginary hands with her own… not going to happen.

She'd been having the most amazing dream. And now she was alone, Jango the only other living being in the room. Her heart raced and her breath came in short, quick gasps. She'd been so close. If the dream had continued, just a minute or two longer, she might have come just from the thought of him touching her.

Mark. My friend.

"Oh, no," she murmured. "No, no, no."

She'd screamed his name. What if he'd heard her? What if he'd woken up to the sound of her voice begging for more?

"Oh, God," she whispered to the empty room.

"Woof!" Jango placed his front paws on the bed and panted down at her.

"Five minutes, boy. I need five minutes." Jango cocked his head to one side. He didn't understand her words, but he knew from the tone of her voice something was bothering her. And he was right.

She needed to get her head on straight and collect her thoughts. How could she face Mark this morning, after last night in her truck, and now this? Waking up screaming his name? He was sleeping in her home, for goodness' sake!

"Stupid dream."

Jango's face was the picture of canine concern as

he nuzzled her. She patted his head. "Maybe he didn't hear me."

Jango licked her face as if to say, *Poor silly woman.*

"You're right. Hard not to hear a woman screaming when there are no doors," she said, pushing back the covers and climbing out of bed. "Who knows what he's thinking now?"

That he wants me so much he's willing to push aside all the reasons one night together is a bad idea and just see where our mutual desire leads?

Jango barked. Downstairs, she heard the chorus of puppies waking and asking to go out, too.

"Okay, I get it, guys. Time to stop thinking about Mark and focus on work." She stripped out of her pajamas and pulled on a pair of jeans, bra and T-shirt. "Everyone is moving into the kennel today. Except you, Jango. You stay with me."

If dogs could smile…

Amy slipped her feet into her shoes and headed for the stairs. Whatever he thought now, she couldn't hide up here all day. Mark had made it clear last night that there were some lines he wouldn't cross. And he was probably right. She couldn't afford to lose him as a friend. Maybe they could both pretend she hadn't screamed his name, her voice sounding suspiciously like a woman on the edge of an orgasm.

Amy tiptoed around the couch and found it empty. She closed her eyes, savoring the relief. Opening them, she glanced at the stack of folded sheets and a note scrawled on the back of a gas station receipt.

Went to give the guys a hand.

"Thank goodness for the Benton brothers," she murmured, leading Jango to the door.

An hour later, after she'd walked and fed the dogs, Amy headed for the kennels. She saw T.J. out in the field finishing up the obstacle course. He'd inflated a small kiddie pool and was filling it with plastic balls. Amy smiled and waved, knowing the puppies would love it. And it would be a good first step to learning to swim with the SEALs.

Inside, she found Mark and Luke putting the finishing touches on the whelping room, the puppies' new home. Nova would have her own quiet space at the other end of the kennel beside Bullet.

"Morning," Mark said from the top of a ladder. He was hanging a speaker in the corner of the room.

"Hey there, Ames," Luke said. "How's the ankle feeling today?"

"Better." She scanned the metal crates, each containing a dog bed. "Are we ready for the puppies?"

"Hanging the last speaker now," Mark said, glancing down at her with a teasing smile. He didn't look the least bit uncomfortable about last night. She felt a tinge of disappointment. Maybe she wanted to see him rocked off his axis after the way he'd touched her on the way home.

"Amy," Mark said. "Mind telling us why the puppies require surround sound?"

"In the beginning I'll play different noises," she explained. "Cars, planes, explosions. I use sound-effects tracks to get them accustomed to different environments so they won't flinch later on."

"I can't imagine my girl reacting to the sound of an explosion," Luke said, referring to Zulu, his K-9 partner. Having chosen the army instead of the navy, Luke worked with the military police's K-9 unit, joining different teams to detect explosives.

"She's well trained," Amy said. Outside, a car door slammed. "I'll go see who's here."

"Probably Gabe," Luke said. "He was running late, but said he'd bring doughnuts."

Amy frowned. She had a good idea why the oldest Benton brother was behind schedule this morning. Eloise. With Jango at her side, Amy headed for the kennel's reception area. Inside, she found Gabe opening a box of doughnut holes and popping one into his mouth. Her cousin stood beside him, setting out coffee, cups and creamer.

"Morning." Amy walked into the room. "Eloise, I didn't expect you today. Don't you have patients to see?"

"Nope." Her cousin turned, her face shining with the happy glow of someone who'd enjoyed her fair share of orgasms the night before. Her eyes were slightly bloodshot from too little sleep. "I'm taking the day off to help you move the puppies."

"Thanks." Amy forced a smile while alarm bells sounded in her head. Eloise rarely did the morning-after thing with the men she dated. But here she was, standing beside Gabe, handing him a cup of coffee. "Why don't we head up to the house and start bringing them down? Gabe, would you mind seeing if T.J. needs a hand in the field?"

"Will do." Her former brother-in-law nodded, grabbing a handful of doughnut holes.

Eloise watched Gabe leave, smiling like a punch-drunk fool. "You know, I think I was right."

"About what?"

"I think Gabe looks the best without his shirt." Eloise selected a doughnut from the box. "Not that I've seen the others, but I can't imagine a man with a better body. His—"

"No, no, no," Amy jumped in. "No details. I saw enough last night in the parking lot. More than enough."

"Sorry. We thought about waiting, but then..." Her cousin shrugged.

"I just hope you know what you're doing, El. He's leaving any day now. And who knows when he'll be back."

Or if he'll come back.

"I don't want to see you get hurt," Amy added. Jango moved to her side, and she started stroking the dog's head.

"It was one night. Just fun. I've known Gabe forever. I feel safe with him. I'll spare you the details, but trusting him allowed me to take risks I wouldn't with another man."

Like being tied up in the front seat of a truck.

"But there is a difference between wild sex and emotional risk," Eloise continued. "I'm not falling in love with Gabe. I'm a big girl, Amy, and I know better. I was torn apart when we lost Darren. But what I felt, it was nothing compared to your loss. I've watched you crawl your way back. After witnessing that, I'd never hand over my heart to a soldier."

"What if you fall in love anyway?" Amy challenged.

Eloise raised an eyebrow. "In one night? Maybe two?"

Amy shook her head. Maybe Eloise was right. A night or two with a man she could trust did not spell true love and heartbreak.

"We're not kids anymore, Amy. You met Darren when we were teenagers. Back then, we had our hearts set on happily-ever-after. But now? I'm building a career. Yes, I'm still a little boy crazy at times. But I have my priorities. One man isn't going to upend my life, believe me."

Her cousin sounded so certain, Amy found herself nodding. And maybe Eloise had a point. What did Amy know about relationships? She was starting all over again. It had never occurred to her that she could write her own rules.

But she could. She wasn't a teenager anymore. Still, she didn't know where to start.

Not with orgasm-inducing fantasies about Mark...

"But Gabe's also a friend," Amy said, knowing she sounded like Mark.

"And now we're friends who get naked together."

Amy frowned, crossing her arms in front of her chest. "It can't be that simple."

"Yes, it can," Eloise said. "Simple and fun. Promise."

BY THREE THAT AFTERNOON, Amy and her team of volunteers had settled the puppies into the whelping room, introduced Nova to her new home and unloaded the rental truck. Leaving her cousin to play with the pups, Amy stood outside in the cool spring air surveying the piles of tent parts, lighting booms and fixtures, outdoor space heaters, tables and chairs. Thank goodness the caterers were handling the dishes and glasses for Saturday's event. With less than forty-eight hours to go, setting all this up with only four men was a tall order.

"Are you guys sure you know how to put the tent together?" Amy asked.

Luke draped his arm over her shoulders. "We've got this. Don't you even think about calling the company back and paying their crew to do this. With the joint efforts of the air force, army and navy working for you, we'll have it up in no time."

Mark glanced up from a pile of metal parts. She swore his jaw tightened when he saw Luke's arm around her.

"You've put so much into this," Mark said. "Let us help you now. Go work with your dogs. When you come back out, we'll have your tent built."

Amy turned to head inside.

"Amy, dear, just a moment," her former mother-in-law called.

Glancing over her shoulder, she spotted Elizabeth Benton marching across the field. She was a tall woman with a full head of gray hair. In her own way, Mrs. Benton—Amy still couldn't think of her as Elizabeth—was just as imposing as her sons, a strong matriarch for her family.

"Mom, I thought you were cooking," T.J. called. "I've been dreaming about your biscuits for months."

"They're in the oven," Mrs. Benton said, heading straight for her. Amy briefly considered escaping inside the kennel, but she knew Mrs. Benton would follow, determined to talk about the menu or the chairs or any of the other small details connected to the dedication.

"Is there a problem?" Amy asked. Maybe the caterers had called to cancel. Or all the guests had decided they had something more important to do.

Mrs. Benton stopped in front of Amy. "I wanted to talk to you about your speech."

"My speech?" Amy repeated. She'd intended to say something about the dogs and her plans for the kennel, but nothing more.

"Before you address the crowd, I would like to say a few words," Mrs. Benton said, her lips forming a warm smile. "I don't know another woman who would go to all this trouble for her late husband. My boy was so devoted. To his country, his family, his beliefs, and to you."

Mrs. Benton's words came from the heart, sending a wave of guilt washing over Amy. Why did part of her fight so hard to make this place hers? She'd known when she put Darren's name on the building that everyone would think she'd opened the kennel to honor him. And there was some truth to that. Darren deserved to be remembered. But worshipped? Placed on a pedestal for his *devotion*?

Darren had been a good man and even better soldier. But Amy knew the truth. He wasn't perfect. And while he'd been dedicated to his team and his country, it hadn't extended to her, not toward the end.

"No one could ask for a more perfect daughter-in-law, Amy," Mrs. Benton continued. "You're like my angel. And I would like a chance, while we have a microphone and a captive audience, to tell everyone how proud I am of you."

Amy tensed. Closing her eyes, she stepped away, needing space before she screamed, *I'm not perfect!* She felt a presence at her side, a strong solid wall of muscle. A hand, familiar and welcome, grasped hers. This time it wasn't Jango who'd come to her rescue, but Mark.

"Sounds like a plan, Mrs. B," Mark said. "But I'm with T.J.—you might want to check on those biscuits. I've been dreaming about them, too."

Elizabeth Benton chuckled. "You boys and your appetites. You'll get your biscuits. And, Amy, please think about it. I would love to say a few words."

She nodded, squeezing Mark's hand. "Of course."

"I'll see you both for dinner," Mrs. Benton said, turning toward the grass field separating the two properties. "Tell Eloise to come, too. I have enough food to feed an army."

"We promise to eat like one," Luke said.

"We'll be there," Mark said, drawing her through the kennel's front door. He kept going, leading her away from the voices to the relative quiet of the veterinary exam room. She could still hear the dogs, but not the Benton brothers.

He released her hand. "Are you okay?"

"I hate the way they see me," she said, her voice wavering. Part of her wanted to scream or cry—maybe both. "I can't stand the fact that Mrs. Benton thinks I'm perfect. I'm not."

"Come here, Amy." Mark drew her into his arms, holding her tight. There was so much comfort here with her face resting against his chest.

"I'm not perfect," she repeated. "And neither was Darren. Did you know he never did the laundry when he was home? Not once. He told his mother he loved her brussels sprouts, when I know for a fact he hated them."

The words came out in a rush. It was as if she'd kept them sewn up inside, but the stitching had come loose.

"He forgot our wedding anniversary," she continued. "More than once. Even when he was stateside, he forgot. And my birthday. And..."

Our wedding vows. The moment he'd gone to bed with another woman, Darren had broken the promises they'd made to each other before he'd become a SEAL, before the never-ending deployments. Before life tore them apart, shattering her faith in him. It took trust to know your husband was fighting half a world away. She'd given it to him. And he'd tossed it aside.

Of course his family didn't know. No one had known

her marriage was crumbling. She'd never said a word, not wanting to tarnish his memory then. She still didn't. What good would it do? They couldn't possibly understand how much she'd wanted Darren to come home. She'd wanted him to witness the downfall of their relationship, or work at her side to pick up the pieces. Even after he'd betrayed her, she'd loved him. She'd wanted to fight for their future.

"I wish they could remember him for who he was, not this god among men," she said. "When he died, I didn't lose a war hero, I lost my husband. And that man, he was not perfect."

"I know."

Amy drew back, looking up into Mark's eyes. Did he? Had Darren told his best friend about his affair?

"I know he had faults," Mark said. "Maybe not about the laundry or the brussels sprouts, but I never saw him as perfect. Still, he was a damn fine friend, brother and son. His family can't help remembering the good."

Wrapping both arms around her, he hugged her tight. "I just wish his family wasn't so determined to bind you to his memory. Because I look around and I see what you've built, and I see a woman who has set out to make a place for herself. I think this kennel is you, Amelia Mae, standing on your own two feet."

His words pushed past the memories and the turmoil they carried with them. For the first time, she felt as if someone saw *her.*

She shifted, wanting to be closer to this man. Maybe it was the lingering desire from her dream, or maybe it was his words, but she couldn't move away. Her hips pressed against him, her fingers moving over his chest, feeling the contours of his muscles. Tracing those hard edges, the sculpted lines of his body, the wild, wanton feelings that had surfaced last night in her truck returned. She wanted to touch more, feel more, experience *more*…

Mark's hands remained frozen on her back, as if he was clinging to friendship territory. But Amy knew they were hovering close to that line. If she rose up on her tiptoes, she could touch her lips to his. If she held him, letting him feel every inch of her body, he might understand her need to steal a kiss, and maybe more, from the only person who understood her. It had been so long. She knew he wanted her. The way his fingers had slipped below her clothes last night. The way he'd looked at her as if it took every ounce of his self-control to say no when he wanted to tear her clothes off and scream yes.

She wanted the Mark from her dream. The man who set her body on fire—

"Amy?"

The sound of his voice—questioning what she was doing—shattered the moment. This wasn't a dream. And he wasn't the man from her fantasies.

She pulled back, her body screaming for her to push forward and claim that kiss. Her hands remained on his chest as the internal battle raged. But he released his hold, his arms falling to his sides, taking the possibility of that kiss with him.

Amy looked down at the concrete floor, knowing it was for the best. Maybe her cousin was right. Amy could write her own rule book when it came to men, relationships, kissing and, God help her, sex. But she hadn't written it yet.

7

AMY'S HANDS BLAZED a path across his chest. Mark didn't know whether to curse his flannel shirt or be grateful for the barrier. Without it, he might do something crazy like claim her mouth and kiss her. Hard.

He stared at her parted lips, wanting to make her his. All it took was her hands on him and her body close to send his imagination running wild. The thought of holding Amy's hips while he pressed into her, feeling her tighten around him… Shit, he wanted that.

His jaw clenched, his hands formed fists at his sides, wishing he could reach out to her again. He'd held her countless times, but never with desire burning so bright they couldn't ignore it.

"I'm sorry," she said, lowering her arms.

"Don't apologize. Not to me." He reached for her hand but changed his mind. He needed the mental picture of Amy wild and unrestrained to fade. If he touched her now, it would only grow stronger.

"We should join the others," he said. Anything that would get them out of this room and away from the sense that he'd jumped over an imaginary boundary, and the fact that he wanted to go even further.

She nodded. "I should find Eloise. Tell her that Mrs. Benton invited her to dinner."

Mark opened the door and held it for Amy. "That wasn't a request. When Mrs. Benton tells you to come to dinner, it's an order."

Amy laughed, but it sounded forced. "No wonder all her boys joined the military."

Mark knew there was more to their decisions, and he had a feeling Amy did, too. But he let the attempt at lighthearted humor follow them down the kennel's corridor to the whelping room. She disappeared inside, and he headed for the front door.

Hand on the knob, Mark paused, closing his eyes. He'd nearly kissed her. Amy—the one woman whose friendship he couldn't afford to lose. If he planned to stay through the opening, live under the same roof, he had to rein in his need. He couldn't screw this up—and he sure as hell couldn't screw her. He knew damn well that wanting something didn't mean you got to have it.

Mark pushed through the door, heading for the half-built tent. "You guys work fast. I didn't expect you'd have the center poles up already."

"Piece of cake once we laid out the canvas," Luke said, holding out a mallet. "Feel like driving in a few pins?"

Mark nodded. He was ready and willing to pound the shit out of something. Taking the tool, he headed for the neatly arranged piles of equipment.

Nearby, Gabe paused, resting his mallet on the ground. "How's Amy?"

"Fine," Mark said.

"She didn't look fine when she headed inside." Gabe raised his arm, wiping his brow with his shirtsleeve.

"She has a lot on her mind," Mark said.

Luke shook his head. "She's working too hard."

"Yeah," T.J. said, frowning. "She hasn't seemed like her old self lately. I still can't believe she stayed off the dance floor last night."

"She hurt her ankle." Mark positioned the pin and raised his mallet to take a swing.

"She looked fine today," Luke said. "I've never seen Amy sidelined."

Mark shrugged. "With that crowd, maybe she didn't want to. Someone might get the wrong idea."

Gabe slowly lowered his mallet without taking a swing. "And think that dancing with Amy would lead to something?"

"No one in town would hit on her," T.J. said.

"I wouldn't be so sure of that," Mark said.

"Amy?" Luke's eyebrows shot up. "She's always been Darren's girl. Everyone around here knows that."

"Darren's not here anymore," T.J. said, his voice tight.

"But we are," Gabe said, and his hand formed a tight fist around his mallet. "If she says something to you, tell us and we'll take care of it. I don't want anyone making her feel uncomfortable."

Mark nodded. He was on the same page. But the reasons he didn't want another man approaching Amy felt selfish after what had happened in the veterinary room.

He glanced from Gabe to T.J. to Luke. Kissing Amy, touching her, helping her find her wild side—that was a one-way ticket to a fight with men he'd always considered family. He mentally added that to the list of reasons to stay away.

An hour later, Mark headed for the hundred-year-old farmhouse that had been like a second home for most of his childhood. Amy had gone ahead with Eloise to help Mrs. Benton in the kitchen. As he approached the brightly lit building, Mark slowed. Through the side windows he could see the Benton brothers smiling and laughing as they carried their mother's home-cooked feast to the table.

When they were growing up, Mrs. Benton had always made enough to feed half the town, as if she expected her boys to bring home strays. He should know. He'd been one of the kids with no place to go but a stool at a run-down diner or an empty apartment with leftovers from his mom's waitressing jobs sitting in the fridge.

Climbing the three wooden steps to the wraparound porch, Mark felt as if he'd stepped back in time. True, he led a team of pararescuemen in Afghanistan. But here, at the Benton family home, he was the quiet kid at the table, soaking up every minute of laughter and warmth as if he could bottle it, take it home and bring it out when he was feeling hungry or lonely.

Mark reached the front door and didn't bother knocking. Not much point when they wouldn't hear him over the conversation and laughter. Instead, he walked right into the fray.

"Just in time," Luke called as he set a steaming dish on the long wooden table. "We're bringing out the last of the food now."

"Smells great." Mark headed through the open pocket doors that separated the formal dining room from the entryway. A lace runner, probably handmade by Mrs. Benton, covered the center of the table. It was overflowing with platters and bowls. Homemade biscuits. Pork roast. Potatoes. Salad. There were more vegetables on the table than he remembered, but he had a feeling that as a kid, he'd ignored those.

Everyone filed in from the kitchen and took their places at the table. Mark claimed an empty spot at the end beside Amy and bowed his head. He listened to Gabe's rushed blessing, knowing the Benton brothers were counting the seconds until they could reach for the biscuits.

"Gabriel James." Elizabeth Benton's voice cut in before her eldest son could wrap up with the words everyone was waiting for: *let's eat.* "You can do better. My family is home, safe and sound at my table. I would like to hear a proper prayer of thanks."

Luke snickered, and Mark suspected Gabe kicked him under the table. But still, the navy SEAL seated at his mother's right side obeyed. When Gabe issued the final go, everyone reached for the food and started filling their plates.

"Mom, what is this?" T.J. held up a bowl full of curly green leaves. Mark had spotted it, too, and decided to pass on it.

"Kale. It's good for you," Mrs. Benton said. "Try it. You'll like it."

"You said the same thing about peas." T.J. eyed the green leaves suspiciously. "I still hate peas."

"Try it," Mrs. Benton repeated, and T.J. reluctantly placed a few pieces on the corner of his plate and passed the bowl to Mark.

"Try it," Amy said, leaning close. Her voice was low, and Mark doubted anyone else heard her as they talked about the upcoming party.

"I need to leave room for biscuits," Mark said.

"I dare you." Her words were barely above a whisper, but he saw the playful gleam in her blue eyes.

He placed two curly leaves on his plate. "Fine."

Amy took the bowl from his hands, her fingers brushing his, sending a red alert to his cock. One touch—that was all it took to set him on edge with need. And he'd been worried things would be awkward after their almost kiss. But there was only an inescapable desire to grab a hold of her and not let go.

"You never could resist a challenge," Amy murmured.

His mind heard the word *challenge* and jumped to a play-by-play of what it would take to make her come.

"Must be what makes you so good at your job," she added.

His job. His team. Right. He felt like a teenager associating every word out of her mouth with sex.

"Hey, Ames." Gabe waved his half-eaten biscuit in Amy's direction. "The tent is supposed to be long and narrow, right?"

"What?" Amy said. "No. It's square. I need to put tables under it. You'll have to start over—"

"Relax, Ames," T.J. jumped in. "It's up and it's square. We put it together after you left this afternoon. Ninety minutes. Luke timed it."

"It's up?" she said, glancing from Gabe to T.J. to Luke. The brothers nodded. And she turned to Mark. "Have you seen it?" she demanded.

"I helped them," he said. "We can swing by and check it out on our way home."

"Okay," Amy said. "But if it is long and narrow, I'm calling the tent crew tomorrow."

"If it doesn't look right, there is something wrong with the materials they sent," Gabe said.

Eloise, seated at Mark's side, turned to Gabe, one eyebrow raised. "You just don't want to admit that the scrawny young guys working for the rental company could build it better."

"They can't." Gabe smiled. "But if you need proof, we could take it down and give them a shot at putting it back up. Time them and see if they beat us."

"No," Amy said. "No one is taking the tent down. I have a list of projects for tomorrow. We have less than forty-eight hours before the ribbon cutting."

The conversation turned to the plans for Saturday, then moved on to various people in town expected to attend. Dinner ended and Mrs. Benton brought out dessert. The Benton brothers joked, taking jabs at each other when they could.

Mark listened and watched, feeling as if he was slipping further and further into the past with each word. How many times had he felt this table shake from one brother kicking the other during dinner? He'd heard Mrs. Benton firmly scold them, her voice filled with equal parts exasperation and love, over and over for years.

Darren and Mark had bonded over a shared love of sports, dogs, and the fact that they were both being raised by a single mother. But that was where the similarities between their home lives ended. Mark's father had been a first-class bastard. Mark didn't know if the man was still alive, and he didn't care.

But Darren's dad had been a steady, strong presence in his boys' young lives until he'd given his for his country. Add to that the fact that the Benton brothers had each other and financial security, thanks to previous generations, and Darren's and Mark's homes might as well have been in different countries.

Mark stared at his pie. His childhood wasn't a place he wanted to revisit.

"I'll clear some of these dishes," Mark said, pushing back from the table. He collected a pile of empty dessert plates and headed for the kitchen. Moving through the familiar space, he set the plates by the sink and went out the back door. On the deck, he drew a deep breath. He just needed a minute and then he could go in, say good-night and walk back to Amy's house.

He sat at the top of the three wooden steps connecting the yard to the deck and stared at the stars. Maybe coming here had been a mistake. He could have stayed on base and then shipped out for another tour as soon as possible. PJs were always in high demand. It probably wouldn't be long before he got back out there.

But Amy had asked him to come to Heart's Landing, so here he was.

Mark stared up at the crescent moon high in the clear night sky. He heard the back door open. Glancing over his shoulder, he spotted her. Amy. Jango trotted past Mark, down the steps and off into the darkness. He heard the door close and felt her claim the empty space beside him on the step.

"It's cold out here," she said, hugging her sweater tight around her middle.

"You don't have to stay," he said. "I can let Jango back in."

"No, the fresh air feels good," she said. "Unless you'd rather be alone. Judging from the way you jumped up to do the dishes, I thought you might have reached your limit."

"Getting close."

She started to rise, and he reached out, resting his hand on her leg. "But I'd like you to stay."

Out of the corner of his eye, he saw her nod as her eyes tracked Jango's movements in the distance. "Can I ask you something?"

Mark moved his hand off her leg, knowing if he didn't do it now, he might give in to temptation and run his fingers up her thigh. He was close to reaching his limit in more ways than one. Lacing his hands in front of him, he rested his forearms on his knees. "Depends."

"Have you been back for a family dinner since Darren died?"

"Yeah, I have."

"But you still miss him more when you're here," she said quietly.

"That's not it." He lifted his hands, running his palms over his face, searching for the right words. "I practically lived in this home as a kid. Eating here brings back memories."

And feelings. Of being the kid who had a place at the table but never quite felt as if he deserved to be there.

"Good ones?" she asked.

"Some." Mark stared out into the night. "But I can't help thinking about the fact that every night I was here, I wasn't with my mom."

"I thought she worked the dinner shift at The Last Stop Diner back when we were in school."

"She did. And breakfast over at the inn. She'd come home and eat a bowl of the Cheerios she kept in the cupboard, so there would be something for me just in case. Then she'd go to bed, sleep for a few hours and do it all over again."

"Everyone in Heart's Landing admired how hard your mom worked to take care of you," she said softly.

"She didn't have a choice. Someone had to pay the rent." She'd never asked him to work, demanding instead that he focus on school and his future. His mother had wanted him to push beyond living for the next paycheck.

"Every night I sat down to eat here, I felt welcome, sure, but also like I didn't belong," he continued. "Tonight took me back."

"I can understand that."

Mark looked up at her. He'd expected her to contradict him, not agree that he'd been an outsider from day one.

"You and I were always the guests," Amy continued. "They made us feel like part of the family, but it's not the same."

"You became family."

"I did." She smiled sadly. "But I think we both know I stayed in Darren's shadow."

"Not anymore."

"No." She playfully elbowed his side. "But don't tell them."

"I won't." Stirring up drama before he deployed again was the last thing he wanted to do.

They fell silent. The Benton brothers' voices drifted out, the sound mingling with the crickets. But the familiar bickering—T.J. giving Gabe shit and Luke jumping into the fray—didn't make him tense up. Sitting out here under the stars, beside a friend who understood how old baggage could rise up at the wrong moments, he felt comfortable. In the distance, dogs barked, their chatter mixing with the voices from inside.

"I should go back in," he said, knowing his brief

reprieve was over. "Say good-night and thank Mrs. Benton."

"No need. I told them you would walk me back. They don't like it when I cross the fields after dark by myself."

Amy stood and headed down the steps, whistling for Jango. The dog appeared out of the darkness. Mark moved to her side, careful to keep space between them.

In the back of his mind, he'd worried that the brief shift between them, the moment when he'd flat-out wanted her, would lead to stilted, awkward exchanges. He looked over at Amy, noting the soft smile on her lips, the way one hand brushed the top of Jango's head. The friendship they'd built over the years was solid. *Thank God for that.* It was like a gift he didn't wholly feel he'd earned, but one he wasn't willing to give back.

"What?" Her gaze met his.

"Just feeling lucky."

"Oh, really?" She raised an eyebrow, and the image of Amy in her underwear filled his mind. He pushed it away.

"Don't go there, Amelia Mae," he warned. He'd held back last night in the truck and today in the exam room, but if pressed, tonight he might give in.

"Go where?" she asked with feigned innocence.

"Amy—"

"Tonight, I think I know just what you need."

His lower half reacted to her words. *Need* was a strong word, but he sure as hell knew he wanted…

No, sweetheart, you don't have a clue.

"Puppies," Amy continued. "They have a way of making the bad memories fade away. Trust me."

Mark forced a laugh, his body still wound up from her words—*I know just what you need.* He allowed her to drag him through the kennel's reception area, down the hall and into the whelping room. He stayed close, watching as her eyes lit up when she spotted the pups jumping and spinning in their metal kennels, overjoyed to see her. Any lingering hint of sadness and self-pity faded. But Mark knew it wasn't because he'd walked into a room full of dogs.

It was Amy.

8

"READY TO PLAY CATCH?"

Amy watched Foxtrot, her most promising pup, spin in a circle barking with excitement as Mark tossed a tennis ball across the room. The puppies raced to claim it, her top contender coming in second to his brother Charlie. Looking back at Mark, she noted his easy smile and relaxed stance. He'd been wound up tight since he'd walked into her house. She liked seeing him like this, playing with her dogs. But part of her was drawn to that tension.

Today, in the veterinary exam room, he'd looked at her as if it took everything he had to let her go without kissing her senseless. Part of her was glad he'd released her. She wasn't ready for where his kisses would lead. First, she'd make a list. Write her own rules. Then she'd return to that moment—and maybe this time she wouldn't hold back.

She watched as he raised his arm, corded muscle visible as his rolled-up sleeve slid to his elbow. In one swift movement, he released the ball, sending the dogs flying across the room a second time.

Amy looked away, focusing on the quiet puppy still resting on her bed. Rosie, the runt of the litter, peacefully watched Mark play with her brothers and sisters as if content with her lot in life. This pup would never make the cut. She would not fight alongside the SEALs, and Rosie seemed fine with that.

Charlie dropped the ball and raced to the whelping room door, barking and jumping up and down. The rest of the puppies followed.

Amy frowned. "Someone's here."

"A little late for company," Mark said, instantly at her side.

A knock sounded on the door.

"You guys in there?" Luke called from the hall.

The Benton brothers. She should have known. Drawing the pups away from the door, she called out, "Yes. Let me get the dogs settled down, and I'll meet you in the front room."

Amy glanced at Mark. "Did they say anything to you about stopping by?"

Mark closed the door to Foxtrot's kennel, tossing the pup a treat. "Nope."

"They're probably heading into town," she said. "But I don't think I'm up for it tonight."

"Your ankle bothering you again?" Mark crossed to the door and held it open for her.

"I don't think I can get away with that excuse two nights in a row. I plan to play the tired card," she said, heading down the hall. "I need my beauty sleep to get through the next couple of days."

"You were born pretty," Mark said. "Sleep has nothing to do with it."

Amy glanced at Mark, waiting for him to shake his

head and admit the words had escaped before he knew what he was saying. But he just held the door open for her.

"Well, sleep has a lot to do with how much I can get done tomorrow," she said before stepping into the reception/office space. Luke, Gabe and Eloise waited inside. Filled with three large, imposing men and the two women, the room felt small despite the lack of furnishings.

"Are you guys headed out?" Amy scanned the flannels and jeans both brothers had worn to construct her tent. Even her cousin still had on her work clothes.

"Nope," Luke said, holding up a six-pack of beer. "Seeing as you missed out on the dancing last night, we decided to bring the party to you tonight. We picked up some local brew."

"We thought you might want to avoid the crowds at the Tall Pines," Gabe said, standing off to the side with one arm around her cousin's waist.

"I think they guessed your ankle wasn't the only thing keeping you off the dance floor," Mark whispered, his breath touching her ear.

"T.J.'s out there right now, hooking up the sound system you ordered for the party." Luke headed for the front door. "We'll mount the speakers tomorrow, but for tonight we set a few on the ground and hooked them up."

"What do you say?" Eloise twirled in a circle. "Up for a dance party? Just us? You already have the tent, and I gave T.J. my best playlist."

As if on cue, Beyoncé's "Single Ladies" filled the cool night air. Amy smiled. She'd been so caught up in the opening and the stress of having the Benton brothers home that she'd forgotten what had drawn her to the Benton family in the first place. These men cared deeply for their friends and family. They wanted to see her happy, smiling and dancing.

"Pass up the chance to see my favorite representatives from the navy, army and air force on the dance floor?" Amy smiled. "Not a chance."

Mark moved to her side. "I hope you're not including me in that group."

"The night's still young." She wanted Mark out there carefree and laughing under the tent, but she also knew he'd prefer to stick to the sidelines. Amy stepped forward and took Luke's hand. "Come on. Let's go."

Luke ran hand in hand with her through the front door to the tent. Amy's laughter bubbled and spilled over as they moved. She'd always loved to dance, but perfecting the steps had never been her top priority. Under this tent, she didn't care if her movements matched the rhythm. Neither did Luke. He looked more like a *Saturday Night Live* skit of a Beyoncé music video than the real deal. If only the army MPs could see him now.

Amy threw back her head and laughed as the song ended. Another chart-topping single with a dance beat and familiar lyrics blasted through the speakers.

"That's my cue to hand you off," Luke said, drawing her close. He sent her twirling right into T.J.'s arms.

Amy caught the youngest Benton brother's hand and moved close enough to be heard over the music. "I hope you got that on video."

T.J. grinned, holding up his smartphone. "Right here. As the fifth born, I learned blackmail from an early age."

She glanced over T.J.'s shoulder to where Luke stood holding his phone up. "I think your brother is trying for his own material."

"Better give him something worth posting on Facebook." Unlike his brother, T.J. found the song's rhythm, moving as if he'd been training for a TV dance competition.

Out of breath, Amy slowed down and went to the sidelines, content to watch the T.J. show unfold. Gabe and Eloise occupied the other, darker half of the tent, dancing slow and close as if they were listening to a different soundtrack.

"You look good out there," Mark said, when she stopped beside him.

"I forgot how much fun these guys are." She glanced at Mark. He stood with one foot crossed over the other, his shoulder leaning against the tent's side pole. In one hand, he held a bottle of beer. While she'd spun and twirled as if she didn't have a care in the world, she'd felt his gaze on her. For so many years, he had been on the edge of the crowd, watching and waiting, always keeping an eye on his friends. But tonight, it felt like more. Hot. Possessive.

"They want to see you happy." Mark nodded to T.J. and Luke, who had both stopped to open a beer.

"I know." She moved closer to Mark. "But not in the same way you do, I'm guessing."

He lowered his drink, his gaze focused on her, so intense she felt a ripple of wanting. "I sure as hell hope not."

She stepped closer, stealing the bottle from his hand. "And just how would you go about making me happy?"

She raised the beer to her lips and took a long drink.

"I think you have a pretty good idea," Mark murmured.

"Tell me."

"Here?"

She nodded, every muscle on edge waiting for him to refuse and walk away. He glanced over her shoulder as the music changed again. And then he placed his hand on her hip, drawing her close.

Lowering his head, his lips touched her ear. "I'd bring you dog toys."

She drew back. "Is that the best you can do?"

"I'm not done yet." He held her gaze, heat replacing the laughter in his brown eyes. "Once the dogs were occupied, I'd lead you into the exam room and finish what we started. I'd kiss you, stripping you down. And I wouldn't stop there. I would explore every damn curve, learning where to touch you to make you scream my name."

"Wow," she murmured. "That's quite the fantasy. Beats a dance party."

"Yeah." Mark stepped away, breaking contacting. "Just a fantasy."

She handed the beer back to Mark, her fingers brushing against his. She wanted to hold them there, prolong the touch. But she drew back, shoving her hands in her pockets. Out here, in the cool night air, his words fresh in her mind, it was easy to wonder about the possibilities.

"I'm making a new list," she said. "A list of rules. I want…"

To kiss him, touch him… She wanted the fantasy.

"I get it, Amy." His jaw tightened, but he didn't look away.

"Amy, get your butt over here and dance," T.J. called as a classic from the eighties blared through the speakers.

"Go," Mark said, lifting his beer to his lips. "This is your night. Dance."

She raised an eyebrow, her hips swaying to the beat as she stepped toward the dancing Benton brothers. "Join me?"

"Out there?" He raised an eyebrow. "No chance. But I'll be watching you."

"One day," she called over her shoulder as she twirled away, joining Luke and T.J. on the makeshift dance floor. "You'll join me. I'll get you off the sidelines."

MARK WATCHED AMY raise her arms over her head, jumping up and down. He'd heard the song before, but he didn't focus on the lyrics—only Amy—his gaze drifting to the rise and fall of her breasts. It was as if her beauty came alive when she was happy. And it went beyond pretty. Amy was hot and sexy in a way that made him want the things he'd spelled out for her.

Amy, her eyes shining bright, her smile wide and genuine, looked over at him. Raising one eyebrow, she held his gaze. Her words from earlier echoed in his mind. Amy wanted to pull him off the sidelines, but where did she want to take him? How far did she want to go?

Mark drained the rest of his beer. He should walk up to the house now and leave Amy to the impromptu party thrown in her honor. But he held back. The song ended, replaced by a classic dance number from their high school days. The ladies on the dance floor screamed with joy and flung themselves into another round of frenzied movement. Mark watched and waited. The way her hips moved—it was pure torture.

Four songs later, Amy rested her hands on her knees as she tried to catch her breath.

"Guys, I'm afraid I have to call it a night. This was a great idea. Thank you. But we have a big day tomorrow."

There was a chorus of good-nights. Eloise pulled Amy close for a hug as Gabe helped his brothers pack up.

"I'll walk you up to the house," Mark said.

Amy looped her arm through his, drawing him in against her side. He stilled, fighting the rising riptide of longing. If he wasn't careful, the Benton brothers would take one look at him and know he wanted Amy in a way that had nothing to do with friendship.

Amy gave a tug, propelling him into motion. Side by side, they walked out of the tent and into the dark night. Jango fell in line at her other side as if he, too, had been waiting and watching Amy, unable to walk away.

Mark looked up at the house, focusing on their destination. She'd left the porch light on, and it glowed like a beacon, welcoming them home.

"Would you like a nightcap?" She released his arm at the front door to pull out her keys.

"What did you have in mind?" Mark asked, knowing it was a bad idea. He should say good-night and head straight for a cold shower.

She opened the door, holding it for Jango. "I have a bottle of whiskey that Eloise left here. But I was thinking of making hot cocoa."

"With marshmallows?" Mark followed her inside, closing the door behind him and turning the bolt.

"Of course." Amy led the way to the kitchen. "You can't have hot cocoa without marshmallows."

"I'm in."

Mark rested his hip against the kitchen counter while

she turned on the kettle and removed the ingredients from the cupboard.

Turning to him, she held up the box. "It's a mix. Nothing fancy."

"Works for me." Right now, everything about her worked for him.

She smiled and went back to work, selecting mugs. The kettle whistled, and she filled the mugs, handing him a cup along with a bag of marshmallows. "Add as many as you want."

Mark added several to his cup before settling into a chair at the kitchen table. Amy sat beside him, raising her mug to her lips.

"Perfect," she said, staring at the melting marshmallows. "You know, in those first few months, I made a cup of cocoa every night. Then I'd sit here and email you."

Mark took a long drink as he pictured her typing away, her eyes filled with the ever-present sorrow he'd seen during their Skype sessions back then. But slowly it had faded.

"You stopped sending memories," he said. "About six months ago."

"You noticed." She lowered the mug, a line of hot chocolate on her upper lip.

His gaze locked on her mouth. He wanted to lean forward and kiss her lips clean.

She shrugged. "I guess I was done living in the past. What about you? Do you still write them down?"

"No." He'd done so in the beginning only to help her. But the truth was he hated reliving his childhood. Thinking about all those days spent hiking with Darren, playing with the Benton family dogs or sitting down to dinner at their table, reminded him how much he'd wished for a family like theirs. Their lives and their happiness seemed so damn effortless. And the worst part was that Darren had understood. From the time they were six years old, right up until when they'd joined the military, each seeking his own path, Darren had tried to make Mark feel as if he belonged, as if he were part of the family.

Amy set her mug down and reached for his hand. "It was a good idea, Mark. It helped me find my way through it all."

He stared at their joined hands. "Must have been, if you started a new list."

Her fingers pressed against his skin. "This one's different."

"I know." He felt her drawing closer.

"I'm writing the rules this time." Her blue eyes lit with excitement as if the power to control her destiny was a present she'd only now begun to unwrap. Unable to look away, Mark saw the moment desire rose up to meet her newfound joy.

He withdrew his hand and reached for his hot cocoa, downing the remains of the lukewarm liquid. "I should go."

Mark pushed back from the table and stood. But Amy followed, stepping close, invading his space. Her hands rose, and before he could move away, he felt her palms touch his face.

He froze, not daring to move. He didn't even blink, just stared down at her. There was a question in her eyes, but it was one he couldn't answer. This had to be her choice. The pulsing need building in him, the desire to wrap his arms around her and taste her—that had no place in this silent conversation.

Her gaze narrowed in on his lips, her body shifting toward his, closing the gap but stopping short of pushing up against him. Rising onto her tiptoes, she touched her lips to his.

Mark closed his eyes, his hands forming tight fists at his sides. Her lips moved over his. He felt her tongue touch his lower lip as if asking for more. Unable to hold back, he gave in, opening his mouth to her kiss, deepening it, making it clear that this kiss was not tied to an offering of friendship and comfort.

Amy's hands moved over his jaw, running up through his hair. Pulling, tugging, holding his mouth tightly against hers. He groaned. She tasted like chocolate—sweet and delicious. He wanted more, so damn much more.

Her fingers ran down the front of his shirt, moving lower and lower. His body hardened, ready and wanting.

The thought of her hand on his cock…

He reached for her wrist, gently drawing her away. She looked up, her blues eyes brimming with uncertainty.

"Amelia Mae." He leaned closer, his lips touching her ear, allowing her to hear the low growl of need in his voice. "Let me know when you've written your rules."

AMY MENTALLY CATALOGED the familiar sounds of her house as her mind raced to catch up with what she'd done. Mark's footsteps on the wood, the sound of the guest room door opening and closing, the click of Jango's nails on the floor as he moved off his dog bed—

I kissed Mark!

She stumbled back a step and sank into her chair. Jango rested his head on her lap, waiting and ready to help her.

"I kissed Mark." Saying the words out loud did little to diminish her shock. Yes, she'd thought about it, wanted it, but doing it? Jango nosed her hand as if unsure if she needed comfort or saving at that moment. She wasn't sure herself.

In the walls, the pipes rattled to life. He'd turned on the shower.

"And I sent him running for a cold shower," she whispered.

A slow grin formed on her lips. She could picture him standing under the cool spray, every muscular inch stripped bare. Her fingers wrapped around the edge of the chair, holding her place, preventing her from invading his shower. The thought of joining him, licking the water off his chest, his abs, nearly propelled her out of the chair and down the hall.

Was he wondering the same thing? Imaging how her mouth would feel on his skin as he stood there?

Maybe he was waiting for her to take charge.

"I could do it," she murmured. For the first time, she felt as if anything was possible, as if she could control her future. "I could interrupt his shower."

But first, she needed to determine the boundaries, find the limits and write her rules. She wanted sex—craved it—but not heartbreak. Not this time.

She stood, her body still on edge with desire, and headed for the hall, Jango at her side. She paused, her gaze locked on the guest bedroom door. The pipes rattled again as he turned off the shower.

Amy turned away. "Bed. Now. Before I do something stupid like offer to towel him dry."

9

MARK WIPED HIS BROW with the handkerchief from his back pocket. For the past few days, winter had been holding on. But today, spring had decided to show her face, raising the temperature a good fifteen degrees while they constructed the last of the dog runs behind the kennel.

"Looks like Amy won't need the space heaters she rented," T.J. said as they carried the roll of wire fencing over to the frame they'd constructed.

"Probably not." Mark set his end of the spool down on the grass and stripped off his flannel shirt, tossing it aside.

"You know, we could finish this tomorrow," T.J. said.

Gabe stopped beside them holding two pairs of wire cutters. "I'm not sure how much longer I'll be here. Might as well do what we can."

Mark nodded. "I don't want to leave Amy with the heavy lifting."

"I thought you were sticking around for a while, Mark," T.J. said. "Your last deployment was what, six months? Aren't you due for some time off?"

Mark stood the spool on its end, preparing to wrap it around the upright posts. "I signed up to fill any shortfalls in upcoming deployments."

"They always need PJs," Gabe said. "If you volunteered, I bet they call you back soon."

Mark nodded, not mentioning his commanding officer knew he wanted to be out there, not sitting on his hands at home. Or at least he had in the past. After last night, and that kiss… Shit, part of him wanted to stick around. But he knew that was not in anyone's best interests. Once Amy started making her list, she'd probably realize she deserved better.

Or maybe for what she had in mind, he'd fit the bill. Amy knew the drill. Men on active duty did not control their schedules. Sure, he'd made this vacation happen, but only because it had come at the end of his tour. If she hadn't asked him to come here, he'd be back at base, waiting to ship out again.

"What about you?" Mark asked T.J. "When are you heading back to Lackland?"

"Wednesday," T.J. said. "But I think Luke's taking two weeks' vacation this time. To spend more time helping out Amy and Mom."

"And you?" Mark nodded toward Gabe as he wrestled with the wire fencing.

"I got a heads-up yesterday," Gabe said tightly. "My team's going wheels up in the next twenty-four to forty-eight hours."

"Shit," T.J. said. "Did you tell Mom?"

"No." Gabe snipped the fencing with the cutters. "And you won't, either."

Mark lowered the spool to the ground. "What about Eloise?"

"It didn't come up." Gabe stepped back, admiring his work. "That girl's looking for a lot of things, but assurances that I'll stick around or come back to her? Not in her game plan."

Mark glanced back at the kennel. What about Amy? Would she require promises? And if she did, would he make them? Words that secured him to one place and one person—those weren't part of his vocabulary, not while he was still with the PJs. And he had no plans to leave. He couldn't. *So that others may live*—those were the words tattooed across his heart.

STANDING UNDER THE TENT directing the caterers as they rushed to set up before the late-afternoon sun slipped behind the mountains, Amy felt as if she was preparing for a grander version of her wedding day. "If I had my way, we would have lined up the chairs in front of the door, cut the ribbon and sent everyone home," she muttered.

"That man over there with the apron?" Eloise, who'd spent the better part of the afternoon helping set things up, pointed to the catering truck. "He said they would be serving hundreds of marionberry thumbprint cookies. And mini grilled cheese sandwiches made with local cheddar."

"So you're coming for the food." Amy chuckled, heading over to the long rectangular table where they'd set out water bottles for the hardworking crew.

"No, I'm coming because you're family and I love you. But I'm excited about the food. And you should be, too. Tomorrow will be fun, and your mother-in-law is picking up the tab for everything she added to your little party."

"It wasn't supposed to be a party," Amy insisted. "I

planned to wrap a ribbon around the building, cut it and give a quick tour to family and friends."

"This will be better." Eloise grabbed her hand and gave it a squeeze just as Gabe walked into the tent.

Her cousin's gaze locked on Gabe's bare chest. "He looks dirty. Maybe he needs a shower. Hmm…how much more do we have to do here?"

"Go." Amy released Eloise's hand. "Just come back early tomorrow morning to help wrap the ribbon around the building."

"Promise." Eloise headed for Gabe. Her cousin took the SEAL's hand and drew him away with a look that promised one long, wild night.

Amy bit her lower lip. *I want that, too.*

She'd stared at her ceiling for hours last night trying to define what she wanted. *Wild, uninhibited sex. And orgasms. So many she'd lose count.*

But then she'd mentally drafted her rule book. If she wanted to safeguard her heart, rule number one was no one who planned to deploy again. She couldn't return to the endless days and months spent waiting. She couldn't follow her cousin's lead, tumble into a soldier's bed without thinking about the morning after.

"If only it was that easy," Amy muttered, shaking her head.

"If what was easy?"

Amy turned to find Mark standing beside her dressed in jeans, a long-sleeved flannel thrown over a blue T-shirt and cowboy boots. Looking at him, feeling his commanding presence, she flushed with the memory of their kiss. Her nipples formed tight peaks beneath her shirt, reminding her that she wanted to feel his hands on her body. She wanted to break the rules she'd crafted last night—or find a loophole.

"Nothing," she said quickly. "How's the fence?"

"We had a few snafus, but it's all in place now." Mark nodded toward Gabe. "His shirt got caught."

"Or he wanted to hightail it out of here with my cousin," Amy said drily.

"Or that." Mark picked a bottle of water off the table. The remaining Benton brothers joined them.

"What's next?" T.J. asked.

Amy surveyed the tables and chairs, the speakers on their stands, the strands of Christmas lights she'd run around the tent's perimeter with her cousin's help. "I think we're done until morning."

"Yeah?" Luke said.

"You guys did a great job," she said sincerely. "Thank you for sacrificing your leave to help me pull this event together and get the kennel set up."

"You ever need anything, we're here," Luke promised. "I speak for all of us. Jeremy, too. If he'd been able to get away, he would have."

Amy smiled. "Thank you."

"You up for pizza in town, Ames?" T.J. asked.

She shook her head. "Not tonight. I need to write up some remarks for tomorrow."

Luke nodded. "See you back here in the morning."

The brothers wandered off, heading toward their family home. Barking sounded from inside the kennel.

"That's my cue," she said, turning to the building. "Dinnertime. Meet you back at the house?"

"Yes," Mark said. "But first, I need to swing by The Last Stop Diner. I'll pick something up for you."

"You don't have to do that," she said.

He reached for her hand, drawing her close. “Yes. I do. I’ll need to borrow your truck to make the trip. Think of dinner as my way of saying thank you.”

“I can think of a few other ways,” she said, knowing she didn’t want food. She wanted a taste of the man standing in front of her. She wished she could brush aside her fears of the morning after.

Heat flared in his brown eyes. “When I get back, I want to hear your ways. Every detail.”

“Yes.”

“Good.” He released her and walked away.

Amy closed her eyes. “Oh, God, what am I doing?”

MARK WALKED INTO The Last Stop, greeted by the familiar smell of seafood chowder. The scent had haunted his childhood, lingering on his mother’s clothes long after she washed them.

He glanced around the brightly lit open space. Pie filled the rotating rack by the register, and vinyl booths lined the walls. Nothing had changed—including many of the staff. Blanche, the owner, waved from her place behind the register. Mark headed over.

“Mark, welcome home! I saved you a stool right by me.” Blanche pointed to the first stool of the ten currently empty seats lining the counter. On the nights Mark hadn’t joined the Benton family for dinner, he had often eaten at the counter, reading or doing his homework while his mother waited tables. Nine times out of ten, Blanche had helped him with his schoolwork.

She picked up her order pad—no fancy computer systems for The Last Stop Diner—and looked at him. “Your usual?”

Mark wasn’t sure the term applied, given he hadn’t

eaten here in a year and a half, but he nodded. "And something for Amy Benton to go. Whatever she usually gets."

"That girl doesn't come in here much anymore. But when she does, she eats like a bird," Blanche said, shaking her head. "I'll have them pack up a cheeseburger, fries and a slice of pie."

She rose, tearing the ticket off her pad, and Mark nearly fell off his chair.

"You've lost weight." *And gained mobility.*

Blanche beamed. "Zumba at the seniors center in town. You should try it sometime."

"Maybe. Amy's been keeping us busy out at her place getting ready for her grand opening."

"It's crazy what she is doing out there." Blanche settled back onto her stool and picked up her knitting. "Raising those attack dogs by herself."

Mark laughed. "Have you told her your thoughts on the matter?"

The lines on Blanche's face drew together. "No. I doubt she wants to hear my opinion."

"She does," Mark said, knowing Amy would find Blanche's words refreshing. "Trust me. But she's a big girl and knows how to handle those dogs better than most men."

"If you say so." Blanche pursed her lips together, shaking her head. "But surrounding herself with those animals? How does she expect to find another husband?"

Mark gazed down at the clean white counter. "I don't think she's looking."

"She can't spend the rest of her life in mourning."

"I don't think she plans to do that, either," he said slowly. But there was a long distance between hot kisses and forever. And replacing Darren? It didn't get much better than a kindhearted, loyal-to-a-fault navy SEAL. Mark wanted her to move on, but couldn't imagine there was a man out there worthy of spending the rest of his life with Amy.

A bell rang, indicating food had been placed in the open window.

"That was fast," Mark said.

"Just your salad." Blanche slid off her stool, setting her knitting aside, and went to retrieve it.

"Salad was never part of my usual." Mark tried to recall if he'd ever eaten a vegetable here.

"If your mama was here, she'd want you to eat your greens," Blanche insisted. "You need to look out for your health."

Mark opened his mouth to tell Blanche that he spent most of his days flying into the fray of war, and The Last Stop's iceberg lettuce covered in ranch dressing with one lonely tomato on the side wasn't going to keep him from getting shot out of the sky. But he quickly thought better of it. Hell, it felt good to have someone give a damn.

AN HOUR LATER, with a to-go bag in hand, Mark walked into the kitchen and found Amy sitting at the table with papers spread out in front of her.

"Last-minute details?" He set the food on the table.

"I'm writing my speech for tomorrow."

He glanced at the sheets of paper. Many of them were balled up and ready for the trash. "Not going so well?"

"No." Resting her elbows on the table, she propped her head in her hands.

"You need to eat." He nudged the bag in her direction. "Blanche sent me home with a burger, fries and pie."

Amy looked up and shook her head. “Thanks, but I’m not hungry. I need to finish this. But what can I say to all those people? They’ll want to hear about Darren, not the puppies. And I’m just not sure…”

“Wing it.” Mark pulled out the chair beside her and sat down.

“I can’t get up there without a plan,” she said. “I need to know what I’m going to say.”

“Then tell the truth.” He took her hand in his. “Explain what this place means to you. Tell them about your dream to train and raise dogs. I think you might find there are more people than you think who look at this place and see you.”

“I hope you’re right.” Amy stared at the papers.

“I am. Don’t worry about it now. You’ll get through tomorrow. I promise.” Mark raised his free hand to her face, running his fingers down her cheek and lifting her chin so she met his gaze. “Right now, I owe you a thank you for sharing your truck.”

She stared at him, and he wished he could read her thoughts. Judging from the hot, wild and enticing gleam in her blue eyes, she was mentally running through scenarios that would more than take the edge off his need to feel and taste every inch of her.

But then she turned away, pulling free from his touch.

“I can’t, Mark,” she said softly. “I wrote my rules, but I don’t know if you’re going to like them.”

He pushed back from the table, reaching for her, drawing her up with him. Pulling her close, wrapping one arm around her waist, he held her, feeling the rise and fall of her chest.

“Try me.”

Amy drew a deep breath, which had the added benefit of pressing her breasts against his chest. He looked down, his hands itching to touch, to explore…

"Rule number four—"

"Wait." His gaze returned to her face. "What happened to the first three?"

"They don't apply if we follow the fourth rule," she said. "No strings and no promises."

Mark raised an eyebrow. No ties between him and Amy? A lifetime of friendship was a damn big string. She was the only person left in Heart's Landing he made promises to—even if there were some he couldn't make to anyone.

"I want to know the other rules," he demanded, holding her tight.

Amy sighed, dropping her chin as her hands ran up his back. "First one, trust. But I do trust you."

"Good." His shoulders tensed at the thought of her giving that up. In his book, trust was never optional—not between friends, teammates or lovers. "And the other two?"

"Number two—no one tied to Darren's memory. And number three—no one in the military."

"I can't change the past." His brow furrowed. Stepping back, he released his hold on her. He didn't want to erase the memory of his best friend, and he wasn't willing to walk away from his future. He needed to return to his team.

Her face fell as she wrapped her arms tightly around herself. He'd witnessed her grief, her determination and her happiness. But seeing her like this? Wanting, but uncertain?

"There is too much history between us. I know that." She drew her lower lip between her teeth. "But the idea of starting something with a stranger…it's thrilling, and at the same time terrifying."

"Thrilling?" Mark felt his chest tighten. He wanted her to move on, but not with some random guy. Not Amy, who should be cherished—who should be *his*.

"I want to cast off the past. Lose myself in the moment. But it's a fantasy. I know that. One big, wild fantasy."

He hated the sad resolve he heard in her voice. She stepped to the side, trying to move around him. He reached for her, unable and unwilling to let her go. He was in the military, and her late husband's friend. He'd move mountains for her, but he couldn't rewrite the facts.

But no strings? A fantasy?

"Amy." He held her arms as he stared down at her. "I'm in."

10

AMY WANTED THIS, craved it. But her mind needed time to process. It was one thing to tease this man. But following through? While the thought of it left her wet and aching, she had reservations. So many ran through her mind it was as if she'd pressed the fast-forward button on her life.

Was she crazy? This was Mark. Could she do this? With him? She almost melted at the thought of his touch, of making love to him, but knowing it would happen?

"Come with me, Amy."

Confusion swirled as Mark took her hand, leading her down the hall to the spare bedroom. With his help, she'd set up a bed and a single chair after transferring the pups to the kennel. But even with the modest furnishings, the space felt barren, so different from the rest of her home.

Mark closed the door and moved behind her. He'd hugged her, held her close countless times. But tonight, his presence dominated the space, demanding all of her senses pay attention to him, tearing her focus away from the questions.

"Mark," she whispered, blindly reaching for him. Her hand brushed his leg, and her world, which had been spinning out of control, steadied.

His fingers grazed the back of her neck, brushing aside her hair. "Close your eyes."

He stepped away, and she felt the loss, her body tensing.

"Keep them closed," he warned.

"Why?"

"Surprise."

The way he said that one word—it sounded like a wicked treat. When he ordered her to close her eyes, when he offered the lure of a surprise, she felt as if she was seeing a new side to the man who had been a part of her life for so long.

Amy heard a door open, footsteps, and then the door closed again. Her body knew the moment he repositioned himself behind her. She fought the urge to lean back and press up against him.

"I want to thrill you." His words rushed over her skin, sending a shiver of excitement coursing through her. Fingers, sure and determined, brushed her cheek. A second later a piece of fabric wrapped around her head, covering her eyes.

"Mark?" She lifted her fingers, exploring the cotton barrier as he tied it tight behind her head.

"I can take it off." His hands pulled her arms down to her sides. Then, finally, he closed the gap, pressing up against her back. "If you want me to."

"No." She leaned into him, feeling the strong, hard planes of his body. "Not yet."

"Pretend for tonight that you are with a stranger."

His words were clear and decisive. "Be wild. Don't be afraid to take whatever you need."

Her mind spun with the possibilities. The freedom to live out her fantasy, knowing she was safe.

Don't be afraid...

Amy turned slowly, careful to keep contact with his body. She'd been plunged into darkness by the blindfold, and he was her anchor. Trailing her fingers up his arms to his neck, then to his face, she touched his lips.

"Kiss me." Her hand moved over his jaw, attempting to draw him closer as her fingers ran through his hair.

Mark's mouth claimed hers, his hands exploring, learning the shape of her body. There was no mistaking this kiss for a friendly gesture. Every touch, every taste, left her body on edge for more. His kiss exploded with passion, blowing away the walls surrounding her day-to-day life, showing her there could be so much more...

But only here, in the darkness, where she dared to be wild.

"Amy," he growled against her lips, pulling back, offering her space to breathe and think.

She could feel him, tense with wanting, waiting for her to lead their friendship down this uncharted path, to reveal her fantasy.

"I'm not sure," she said, hating the hesitation in her voice. Damn it, she *wanted* this.

Mark held her tight, his hands on her hips. His forehead rested against hers. "We can stop. Walk away now. But, Amy, I'm dying to see you move."

He released her right hip, and she heard the rustle of his clothes. And then—music.

The slow rhythm of drums, building, growing stronger, picking up speed, but not out of control.

There were no vocals, just the pulsing beat blended with instruments.

"The quality is not great. I'm playing it on my phone." She felt him move away, taking the music with him. "But will you dance?"

She followed the sound of his voice, turning and reaching for him. "You'll join me?"

"Yes."

His hand caught hers, drawing her close again. Since she was unable to see, her other senses came alive. Every touch was magnified. The drums sounded as if they were growing louder. Her hips moved, rocking to the beat. She raised her arms over her head, still holding his hand. She spun in a circle. Then her body found the pulse of the drums again. She moved freely with it.

"I must look—"

"So damn sexy," he cut in, his voice low and rough.

"Oh." Her movements slowed, her mind turning over those words. Sexy and sensual, living in the moment for the pure pleasure of it—that wasn't her. But maybe just for tonight, here with him, lost in this fantasy world.

"Don't stop." It was spoken as a command, but with a hint of pleading.

"You said you would join me." She found his chest, running her hands down over his rock-hard stomach, feeling the muscles she'd admired so many months ago through her computer screen. Grabbing a hold of his hips, she drew him near, demanding that he join her.

Widening his stance, capturing her leg between his as he held her close, Mark began to move. His body swayed in time with the music. Taking the lead, he guided her in a circle, maintaining contact always, his hands exploring, touching her lower back, traveling up to her waist, mapping her, but never losing the beat.

"You can dance," she whispered, her body on fire.

"For you," he said, his voice tight. "Yes."

His words were like a drug—intoxicating, leading her down the path to wanting more. Allowing her core to brush up against his thigh, she felt herself growing wet with need. And she knew from the hardness brushing against her lower stomach that he felt it, too.

His hands found her breasts, and she arched, pressing her nipples against his palms. The drums sped up, growing louder, transforming from sensual to frantic. Amy felt her need growing with the music. She reached for the buttons of his flannel shirt. She released the first, ran her fingers down to the second as she continued to dance. Then the third and fourth, before she grew frustrated, pulling at his clothes.

Mark came to her rescue, removing his shirt. Her palms rested against his bare skin, feeling the dusting of hair. The music grew more frenzied as if pushing them forward. She found the button at the top of his jeans just as his hands tugged at her shirt.

Their movements matched the music as they stripped away clothes, each struggling to feel the other, but barely taking the time to explore before tearing off another layer until there was nothing between them—no barriers apart from her blindfold. The music peaked, the drumming reaching an impossible speed. And then it stopped.

Amy froze and reality descended. She stood naked and blindfolded, touching every inch of Mark's body. There was no going back from this, not now.

But then the music interrupted, the track starting at the beginning, filling the space with an even rhythm.

She knew now that it would grow and build until it exploded. Her pulse sped up. Excited. Ready.

As if he'd sensed her willingness to follow their dance to completion, Mark stepped back, holding her naked body close, taking her with him. He came to an abrupt halt, breaking free from the rhythm as he turned them around. Gently, he stepped into her, urging her back. She felt soft, cotton fabric against the back of her legs.

The bed. Amy stilled, her pulse the only part of her keeping time with the music. He guided her down, her body sinking into the feather bed covering the firm mattress beneath. Her legs hung over the edge.

"Mark?" she said, her voice barely audible over the music. Where was he? She couldn't feel him. Her hands ran over the duvet cover, searching.

"I'm right here." She felt the words against her ear. His legs brushed up against hers, and she felt him hovering over her.

His lips kissed her jaw, her neck, the slope of her breast, moving in time with the drums, dancing over her skin. He caught her breast in his mouth, his tongue swirling over her nipple. Pleasure ignited, rushing over her, through her. Part of her wanted to watch him, see the tension in his muscles as he held his torso above hers, licking and kissing his way down from her breasts, lower and lower…

But the blindfold offered the pretense of safety. This was a game, a fantasy—nothing more. It added an element of kink that turned her on, allowing her to imagine a gorgeous stranger worshipping her body, not a friend bound to the parts of her life she wished to set aside, at least for tonight. It reminded her that she was allowed this pleasure.

His hands touched her knees, drawing them apart. She didn't need to see to know he'd lowered down to the floor, positioning his broad shoulders between her legs. Amy bit her lip, loving and hating the anticipation at the same time.

Fingers moved to her inner thighs. The drums raced forward, seemingly a step ahead of them. Amy lifted her hips off the mattress silently begging, her fingers clutching the comforter at her sides. His thumb brushed over her.

"I'm going to make you come," he said as if she needed a warning, as if she wasn't so far lost in her own need, she'd never find her way back without him.

His tongue ran over her, drawing forth a low moan. If he heard her, he didn't offer any indication. The licking, sucking, the occasional nip of his teeth continued. She felt his finger at her entrance. He slipped inside, filling her. Teasing her with his mouth at the same time, he pushed her closer and closer, her body racing to meet the drums' frantic pace. The music reached its pinnacle, taking her with it. The track ended leaving only her cries.

"Oh, God! Yes, yes, yes!"

Panting, her body humming from head to toe, she was vaguely aware of the music starting again. The bed shifted beside her, and she turned her head, knowing Mark was there by her side even though she couldn't see him.

"Are you okay?" he asked, his voice soft and gentle.

"Hmm." It was all she managed.

His fingers brushed her cheek, moving to the edge of the blindfold as if he wanted to peek beneath.

"No," she said. His hand stopped, and then disappeared. "Not yet. We're not done."

And she wasn't ready to open her eyes to reality. She wanted to stay here, surrounded by music, pleasure, lost in the dreamlike feel of this moment.

Amy rolled onto her side, facing Mark though she couldn't see him. She reached out, her hand finding his arm. It was her turn to touch and explore, to drive him wild. She gave him a little push, silently directing him to lie on his back. Feeling her way, she slid her body over his, resting one knee on either side of his hips, trapping the hard length of him beneath her core. Hovering over him, sensing the tightly coiled tension coursing through him waiting to explode—she'd never felt this powerful.

"My turn," she murmured. "To make you scream."

AMY HAD BEEN part of his life for years, but he'd never seen her like this—naked and straddling his cock, her face flushed from coming against his mouth. It was the most erotic sight he'd ever witnessed. The way she licked her lips, pursing them together as she gently tilted her pelvis, increasing the pressure until he was close to exploding. Her breasts…

Mark groaned, reaching up to run his thumb over one nipple. She leaned into his touch, and it was all the encouragement he needed to reach his other hand up.

It was a damn good thing she'd kept the blindfold on, instead of letting him look under to see if she was all right. Without it, she'd realize that when he looked at her, his emotions surged. The desire to make her his rose up beside the need to please her. Making Amy happy—that had to come before everything else.

Staring up at her, he homed in on that need. He massaged her breasts, his hands working in time with the music, his focus on the soft sounds she made when he traced circles around her nipples or pinched them between his thumb and finger. The drumming grew frenzied, and the shallow movements of her hips followed. But when the song ended, she froze.

"More, I want more," she said, her voice more demanding than pleading.

"Right there with you," he ground out.

His hips thrust up into her, desperate for the friction. He needed to feel her soft body moving back and forth against him. The song started again. This time Amy lifted up slightly, her hand reaching for him, stroking him and positioning him at her entrance.

He knew this dance. But first…

Mark stilled her hips, holding her tight against the hard ridge of his cock. "I need a condom."

"Oh," she said, shifting off him and onto the bed. "Right."

He felt the uninhibited woman who'd been riding him moments earlier slipping away. Mark scrambled to his rucksack, digging through it to find the ziplock bag holding his toothbrush, shampoo and—thank God—a condom. He tore the wrapper, quickly covering himself before heading back to the bed.

"Lie down," he said softly, relieved to see her still wearing the blindfold. He had a feeling the minute she took it off, it was game over.

Amy obeyed, lowering herself slowly, feeling her way, careful not to hang off the edge. Mark covered her body, resting his weight on his elbows. She'd retreated too far. He wanted her mindless with pleasure, ready to ride straight into another orgasm, not thinking and wondering.

Lowering his lips to hers, he kissed her. Gently at

first, pulling her back to that place where she wanted to move with abandon. He deepened the kiss and felt her hips rise up, greeting him.

"Mark, please," she begged, her mouth moving against his. She reached between them, grabbing hold of him, positioning him between her splayed legs for a second time.

The last vestiges of logic slipped away as he thrust into her. He moved with the rhythm, not once losing the beat. Yes, he knew this dance. But with Amy beneath him, saying his name over and over—special didn't begin to cover it.

The drumming became impossibly fast, nearing the end.

"Come with me," she said.

He felt her tighten, her nails digging into his back as he exploded, the orgasm ripping through him, the feeling of this moment imprinting on his mind.

And then the song ended.

Mark rolled off her, lying by her side. Amy's body touched his. He didn't want to move, to break this moment.

Amy sat up, crossing her legs in front of her. His fingers brushed her thigh, his body still craving a physical connection as he watched her. She raised her arms up, her fingers pulling at the knot in the blindfold.

"Can I take this off now?"

"Of course." He sat up, helping her undo the fabric.

Lowering the scarf he'd pulled from her hall closet down to her lap, she turned to him, blinking as her eyes adjusted. "Hi," she said softly.

He brushed a strand of hair away from her face. "Hi."

"What is this? The music?"

"Not sure what it's called. I use it for running sprints." Though he doubted he'd ever be able to hear it again without remembering her.

"That was quite a workout." She slid off the bed and began pulling on her clothes. "Thank you."

"You're leaving?" Mark swung his legs over the edge of the bed. Every muscle in his body begged him to stop her, keep her here with him.

"I need to follow my rules, Mark." She picked up his cell phone and held it out to him. "I know you said one night would never be enough, but it has to be."

Mark took the phone, silencing the track. "I get it."

He wanted to say to hell with the rules, but she was right. One night of comfort—a way for her to reclaim a lost part of her life—that's all this was.

The door closed behind her, and he fought back the urge to go after her. Because knowing it was only one night didn't change the unsettling sensation in his gut that what they'd shared was so much more.

11

AMY OPENED ONE EYE and stared at the Belgian Malinois sitting on his haunches, his tail thumping the ground.

She rolled to her side. "I'm getting up. I promise."

Tossing back the covers, she sat up and stretched. Every inch of her body hummed with the memory of last night. She waited for guilt to descend. She'd made love to Darren's best friend. Blindfolded. And she felt… happy.

Would he feel the same? Her fingers drummed on the sheets. She should talk to him before the madness of opening day began—

Woof! Woof!

"Okay, okay. You need to go out. I hear you." She stood, stripping out of her pajamas and pulling on her work clothes. After she'd taken care of the dogs and finished setting up, she'd change into the red dress she'd ordered for today.

Downstairs, Amy opened the front door, letting Jango race past her to find a tree. Knowing he'd come around to the back, she headed for the kitchen. She found Mark leaning against the counter and eating fries from the to-go container he'd brought home last night.

She paused in the entryway. With the long-sleeved flannel thrown over a white T-shirt, the cargo pants and work boots, he looked exactly the same. But now she knew what lay beneath his ordinary clothes. She knew how his skin felt. She knew how he moved.

A flood of wanting replaced her happy morning-after glow. Seeing Mark, she wished they could slip away and hide in her spare bedroom, blocking out the rest of the world with a blindfold and mind-numbing pleasure.

"Morning." His smile was warm and welcoming, drawing her into the room.

"Cold fries, the breakfast of champions?" she teased, moving to the closet where she kept Jango's food.

"Hey, I heated them up," he said. "And it was this or dog food. Your cabinets are bare."

"I haven't had time for grocery shopping lately," she said, scooping the food into the dog bowl.

"I'll take you after the opening."

He said the words as if his place was here, helping her, becoming a part of her life. Amy rose slowly. "Mark, about last night..."

His expression turned serious. "Rule number five. No regrets. Not between us."

Relief washed over her. She didn't want him to feel remorse for what had happened.

"I like that one," she said softly. "And you don't have to take me shopping."

"You either let me or I tell Elizabeth Benton that the only thing in your cabinets was a box of cereal so stale I wouldn't touch it."

She pictured her well-intentioned mother-in-law

checking her kitchen for food every few weeks. "You win. I'll go."

"And take this." Mark held out the to-go container. "Eat. You'll need your strength to face your two hundred guests."

Amy groaned, closing her eyes. "Don't remind me."

"Hey," he said, holding a fry to her lips. "You'll get through this."

She nodded, knowing he was right. She'd survive today. She didn't have a choice.

Thirty minutes later, Amy was securing blue ribbon to the side of the building. Working beside her, T.J. unwound the spool as she ran her hand over the satin, pressing it flat. They rounded the corner heading for the front door, where Amy planned to hang a giant blue bow. In two hours, the first guests would arrive.

Glancing at the tent, she spotted Mark on a ladder adjusting the speakers. It was warm again today, and he'd cast off his flannel shirt. With his arms raised overhead, his T-shirt rose up revealing his toned lower abdomen. She wanted to run her lips over the contours of his sculpted body. She wanted another night, blindfolded in his bed…

Her face heated. Carrying a secret with her through the day was nothing new. But this one threatened to melt her from the inside out, leaving her wet and needy from the memory of their very naughty dance. She turned away, running her hands back and forth over the ribbon.

"Are you okay, Ames?" T.J. glanced over at her.

"Nervous, that's all."

Country music filled the tent. It wasn't the same as last night, not even close, but she heard the drums in the background, and her mind turned to Mark pressing up against her. Naked. The ribbon was soft to the touch, but his skin felt better.

"About getting everything ready," she added quickly, feeling her cheeks heat up.

T.J. studied her a moment longer as if trying to decide if he should probe further. But then he looked away, and Amy breathed a sigh of relief.

"Looks like the stragglers are finally here." T.J. nodded to the open field connecting her property to the Benton family home. "With the added manpower, we'll be ahead of schedule in no time."

Amy spotted Gabe and her cousin walking briskly through the freshly cut grass. They'd been glued together for the past few days. But now they were maintaining their distance. Warning bells went off in Amy's mind. If Gabe had hurt her…

But no, this was Eloise. Her cousin steered clear of serious. She definitely knew more about how to have a fling than Amy.

They approached the tent, heading straight for her and T.J.

"About time you guys showed up," T.J. called. "Did you at least bring doughnuts?"

Gabe shook his head. No one would label Gabe the easygoing, fun-loving brother, but Amy would generally stop short of severe. Not today, she thought, stepping away from the ribbon, her concern brewing.

Gabe stopped in front of her. "Amy, I'm sorry. I have to leave. My team's going wheels up. For all I know, it is just a training exercise, but I have to go."

Beside her, T.J. let out a soft curse. But Amy just nodded, feeling the color draining from her face as her body switched to autopilot. She'd heard those words so many times. *I have to go. Just a training exercise.* But there was always a chance his SEAL team would be headed for the latest conflict. And some of them might not come home.

"I understand," she said, wrapping her arms around Gabe, hugging him tight. The familiar, helpless feeling of saying goodbye to a man who might never return surfaced, and she knew it would linger.

Under the tent, the music stopped. She spotted Mark, his expression grim. He might not know yet, but he'd guessed. He'd gone through these motions so many times.

"If there was any way to stay for the opening and dedication, I would," Gabe said, drawing back and releasing her.

"I know." She stepped away as Mrs. Benton approached, her face lined with worry. "I'll let you say your goodbyes."

Amy signaled for Jango, and he moved to her side, pressing against her leg, offering support.

"Amy, wait," her cousin called. "I'll go with you. Give you a hand."

"Eloise, stay," she said. "I can manage."

"No." Eloise turned to Gabe, offering a smile as she gave him a quick hug and a kiss on the cheek. "Be safe out there. I'll see you when you're back in town."

Gabe nodded, and Amy could see the relief on his face that he'd escaped a long, tearful goodbye. But anything more than a quick kiss would violate the rules of a fling, Amy thought ruefully. And Eloise always stuck to the playbook when it came to men. She even made it look easy.

Maybe if Amy followed similar guidelines with Mark,

she could have another night, maybe more, and still be spared the heartache when he left. Jango nuzzled her leg, and she blindly reached for him, running her hand over his head. Or maybe she should have followed the no-military-men rule without exceptions.

"El, I need to go." Amy turned and headed for the house. If she stayed, she might fall apart. And she didn't have time to pull herself back together before the guests arrived.

Eloise caught up with her halfway to the house, not saying a word as they approached the back door. Amy glanced at her cousin and saw one lone tear running down her cheek. Eloise quickly wiped it away. Amy looked at the house. Almost there.

Inside, she found two glasses and filled them with water from the kitchen sink. Turning, she held one out to her cousin.

"Tell me the truth, Eloise. Are you okay?"

"I checked the news on my phone. After he told me." Eloise accepted the water, holding it tight between her hands. "Aid workers are trapped in Syria. There are mounting tensions in some small country in Africa I had never heard of and—"

"Guessing doesn't help," Amy said quietly. "Trust me."

"How did you do this over and over?" Eloise demanded. "And not lose your mind?"

"I didn't have a choice. I married a man who wanted to serve his country. He firmly believed that every time he deployed, it was worth risking his life."

"Did you?"

Amy took a long drink of water, turning the question over and over. "When I stepped back and looked at those headlines, yes, I did. Those aid workers in the news, what were they doing?"

"Rescuing children from a small village torn apart by war."

"After Darren left, I would watch the news for the first week, telling myself he was saving the world. It was greedy to want him home with me when he could be out there helping others. But some days, I woke up and I wanted to be selfish." Amy shrugged. "I wished I could have my husband home safe and let someone else save the world. I loved him, and I hated the thought of losing him."

Amy drained the rest of her glass and set it aside. "I know you said you wouldn't, but did you fall in love with Gabe?"

"No." Eloise's eyes widened. "Of course not. I care about him. We've been friends for years. But we only spent a couple of nights together. I just… I wasn't ready to let him go. I'm usually the one who ends things, not the other way around."

Amy nodded, knowing she should feel relieved that her cousin had not fallen head over heels for a man whose duty required that he walk away at a moment's notice. But inside she knew this was a warning. Mark was leaving, too. If losing her temporary lover shook her cousin, what would happen to Amy when Mark left? They'd said no strings, no promises, but saying the words didn't mean her heart believed them.

12

An hour later, Amy stood by the buffet table with a smile plastered on her face. She'd changed into her red sheath dress, matching blazer, stockings and simple black heels. Her blond hair was pulled up into a twist that looked effortless despite the dozens of pins required to keep it in place. In her hand, she held a plate overflowing with cookies. Moving through the crowded space, she felt as if she were navigating a nightmare.

"There you are." Her mother-in-law grabbed her arm, pulling her toward a group of familiar faces. "You remember Alan and Marie Hardwick from church?"

"Of course." Amy held out her free hand. "Thank you for coming."

"We're so proud of you. Building this all by yourself," Marie Hardwick said.

"Oh, I had lots of help," Amy said, nodding to her former mother-in-law.

"Of course you did." Marie kept a hold of Amy's hand, leaning closer. "Have you thought about what you're going to do with the profits?"

Amy felt her hand holding the dessert plate dip, but

caught herself before she dropped the jam-filled cookies on Marie Hardwick's shoes.

"The profits?" she repeated. From breeding dogs? She hoped that after expenses she would break even. But that was a big if, considering not all of the pups would be like Foxtrot and his brother Charlie. Only the top dogs would sell to the military or even police departments. *If* she saw profits from the business, enough to cover her expenses and then some, she planned to reinvest the money, maybe hire another trainer or buy a second female dog with strong bloodlines from overseas. Or maybe she would just be lucky to afford dog food and groceries.

"Our son is a lawyer in Portland, and he works with small businesses. Kevin. He was two years behind you in school. I'm sure he would be willing to help you start a charity fund."

Mrs. Hardwick released her hand, and Amy's arms dropped to her sides. The cookies fell to the grass. They wanted her to give away the money she made from her business?

"We hadn't given it much thought," her mother-in-law said, filling the silence. "We've been so busy preparing for today."

Amy stared at the broken cookies, the jam sticking to the blades of grass. "If you'll excuse me," she said, reaching for Jango's collar. "I don't want him to be tempted. By the cookies."

The Hardwicks looked down at Jango and then up at her, their faces lined with sympathy.

"I'm sorry, dear," Marie said. "I should have waited until another time. Today must be so hard for you."

"It's not that," Amy began. But what could she say

that didn't make her sound awful and selfish? "Jango's gluten-free. The cookies will make him ill."

Amy fled before the Hardwicks' sympathy turned to confusion. She moved through the crowd, not stopping or making eye contact. The space grew smaller and smaller, shrinking, tightening, pushing the people closer. It was like fighting through a maze.

Amy reached the edge of the tent and wrapped her hand around a tent pole to keep herself from tumbling over. From here, she could hear the dogs barking in the kennel, begging to join the party, to play, to chase. She wanted to join them, hold them close, forget this day that had started with a happiness she hadn't felt in so long and descended into this confused, trapped place.

"Amy." A hand touched her shoulder, and she flinched. The deep, familiar voice moved closer, surrounding her, as if trying to protect her from the people under the tent. "It's just me. Mark."

She turned to him—Mark—the one person who understood her, who didn't expect perfection.

"Hey, you don't look so hot," he said, keeping his hand on her shoulder.

"Thanks," she said. "Now I feel ready to get up in front of hundreds of people."

"You're beautiful, and red was a great choice," he said, giving her shoulder a light squeeze. "But you look pale, Amy. And you were running away from your party."

Amy stared past him into the tent. "I dropped a plate of cookies."

"I can see how that would be upsetting," he said, leaning close. "I know how hungry you must be, seeing as you refused to eat the leftover fries this morning, but that doesn't mean you need to leave."

Amy laughed, the panic of the event gradually receding.

"That's better. I like seeing you happy." His thumb traced small circles over her collarbone, dipping below the high neckline of her dress.

"You can't," she said, her voice barely above a whisper. "If someone sees."

"My hand on your shoulder?" He raised an eyebrow.

"It's more," she said, feeling his thumb run across the top of her breast.

"You and I know that, but no else. It's our secret." He withdrew his hand. "And I think we're safe for now."

Amy stared into his brown eyes. This man possessed a seemingly endless reserve of strength, always there for her when she needed to lean on someone. But he wasn't permanent. She couldn't forget that.

"You're leaving."

He shook his head. "No, I'll stay until the end. I already told Mrs. Benton I would help clean up."

"I didn't mean the party," she said. "You're leaving Heart's Landing, redeploying."

"Not right now, Amy. Today, I'm here for you. Promise."

They'd said no promises, no strings, but this was one she wanted to keep, holding it close, taking comfort from those words. She wished she could take his hand and lead him away from all of this—

"Welcome!"

Amy jumped at the sound of her mother-in-law's voice pouring through the speakers. Jango pushed up against Amy's leg, steadying her.

"Guess it's showtime." Mark stepped to the side. "Ready?"

Shoulders back, Amy headed for the front of the tent determined to move past this grand spectacle.

"I'd like to introduce you to my daughter-in-law, Amy Benton," Elizabeth continued. "Years ago, a shared love of dogs drew Amy and Darren together. I know many of you here today have boarded your pets with her or turned to Amy for help training your four-legged friends. I hope you will continue to support her efforts to make this business a success."

Amy stumbled, quickly regaining her footing as she approached the big blue bow on the kennel's front door. Her mother-in-law placed the microphone in her hand, leaning close.

"Thank you," Elizabeth murmured.

As the older woman whom Amy had considered a second mother for so many years stepped away, Amy noted the gleam of unspilled tears in her eyes. There were lines on her face, visible up close despite Elizabeth Benton's carefully applied makeup, that spoke to years of worry, first for her husband and then her boys.

"You're welcome," Amy said, feeling the truth behind those words for the first time. She had not set out to build this place as an ever-present link to her late husband, but she could pretend for one more day. Amy could take her place on that pedestal of perfection alongside the imperfect man she had loved and lost. And she would—for Elizabeth Benton, the woman who'd spent her life worrying and waiting. Amy could choose to never travel that path again. But this mother of five was locked into a future of not knowing if her sons were in danger or if they would return.

"Hello," Amy began, pausing at the sound of her voice through the speakers. It was clear and strong. Looking out at the crowd, she spotted Luke and T.J., who stood in the front row, the medals on their dress uniforms sparkling under the strands of Christmas lights.

Don't be selfish.

"Three years ago, when I first opened my K-9 boarding and training business, I had my husband's full support. But then most of you knew Darren. He came from a family of dog lovers. Some of them are here today." She paused, gesturing to the Benton brothers.

"He joined the navy determined to become a SEAL. Once he did that, he set his sights on becoming a war dog handler. He believed he could better serve his country with a four-legged teammate at his side. And Darren, well, he crushed every goal he ever set for himself," she continued.

"One night, while he was home on leave, we came up with a plan to breed future war dogs." *My plan,* she thought, knowing she was entering the gray area between fact and fiction. But she forced a smile and pressed on.

"After Darren gave his life in service of his country, I decided to turn the breeding and training center into a reality. I wanted to provide the best dogs. Animals that would keep the soldiers at their sides safe in war zones, where that feels like a foreign concept."

Applause punctuated her words, growing and becoming louder. She saw the pride on Elizabeth Benton's face. Amy's gaze traveled through the crowd, landing on Mark. He'd remained in the back of the crowd, leaning against a tent pole. Her resolve faltered.

She'd danced naked for him last night, and she'd

woken up today without regrets. The woman who'd done that—she was not a saint. Not even close. And that woman should not be up here, pretending.

She quickly looked away from Mark. No one knew. It was their secret. But how many more truths could she keep under lock and key before the pressure of carrying them from dawn to dusk broke her?

She'd wanted to find her place outside of Darren's shadow, but now that she was standing in the spotlight, it felt as if she was risking too much, as if standing here illuminated fears she preferred to ignore.

13

MARK KNEW WHEN a mission had headed south. He'd seen it often, when fallen soldiers—out of their minds with pain, shaken by the recent memory of an attack—tried to escape the helicopter or fight the PJs working to save them.

Amy faltered, her smile and confidence slipping away. He saw it in her eyes, the way she glanced at the open field outside the tent. She'd delivered the performance everyone expected, the one that would offer the Benton family comfort. But he had a feeling she could only maintain the lie for so long.

Mark pushed off the tent pole and headed for her, sticking to the outskirts of the gathered crowd. He needed to get to Amy, to divert the focus and steal her away from here. She'd been through so much, worked so damn hard to pull her life together; she didn't owe anyone an explanation.

She raised the microphone again. "I'm sorry. When I think about what these dogs are capable of, how they can help by detecting explosives, and so much more, I..." She pursed her lips together.

"Keeping those men safe, sending them home to their families, that is important to me," she added softly.

The soft murmur of voices started as a whisper and grew to a roar, all in agreement. Applause followed, reminding him that everyone here today wished Darren's last mission had resulted in a homecoming instead of a funeral.

Mark halted, steps from the front of the tent and Amy. He wanted Darren here, alive and breathing. But if Darren had lived, Amy would belong to his friend. Last night would never have happened.

No regrets. He'd written that rule. But damn, he felt torn between a need to help this brave, beautiful woman move forward, to honor their mutual attraction, and loyalty to the man who had been his closest friend.

One glance at this crowd drove home the fact that Darren was a good person, loved by so many. And Mark? Shit, he'd never merit this reception. No one would put his name on a building.

Because he'd never let anyone get that close, not when he could lose his life on a mission.

Mark looked back at Amy. The panic haunted her. He could see it in her eyes. But she was pushing through, picking up the oversize scissors ordered for today. Raising them with a forced smile, Amy cut the wide blue ribbon in one swift motion.

Men and women rushed forward, threatening to box her in and shower her with congratulations. Mark moved to the side, determined to remain close, prepared to extract her.

"If you'll excuse me," Amy said quickly, stepping away. "I need a minute."

Stepping over the ribbon, she opened the door and

disappeared inside. Mark followed, determined to search her out. The door slammed behind him.

"Amy," he called.

He scanned the empty hall as he moved farther into the building. He found her standing with her back pressed against the wall, her head back, eyes closed.

He slowed, moving to her side, fighting the urge to draw her into his arms. "It's over."

"It was a lie." She turned and headed down the hall, moving farther away from the voices outside. "So many damn lies."

Mark followed, stopping beside her when they reached the door to the veterinary room.

"I lied to you this morning. And last night." She opened the door, leading the way inside. "I didn't want just one night. A fantasy," she said, speaking quickly.

"Amy." He placed his hands on her shoulders and turned her to face him "What do you want? Tell me now."

She touched his arms, running her hands up to his shoulders, mapping the contours of his neck until she reached his face. "You. I want you for myself."

"I'm here for you, Amy. It's okay to want something for yourself."

"Is it?" She stepped closer, pressing her body flush against his.

"Hell, yes." *As long as that something is me.*

"Please, kiss me, Mark." Her blue eyes stared up at him, her nails digging into his shoulders. She rose up on her tiptoes, running her fingers through his hair as she drew his mouth down to meet hers. Amy kissed him long and hard. His hands moved to her hips, drawing her against him, letting her feel how much he wanted her.

But even through the thick cinder-block walls he could hear the hundreds of well-intentioned people gathered to see her. They'd watched her slip inside the building, and most had witnessed Mark chasing after her. If they didn't come back soon, someone would come looking for them.

He pulled back. "Amy, I want this, too. But there are two hundred people here. You need to go back."

"Not yet." She guided his jacket off his shoulders and tossed it aside. Her hand moved to his chest, toying with the buttons on his shirt. "I can't stand to spend another minute up there on that pedestal of perfection. I want to be here with you."

He couldn't say no to her. Not to Amy. If she needed him, if she wanted him here, he'd stay. He pushed aside the voice in the back of his mind that warned she was seeking an escape, nothing more.

Hell, that should work for him. He didn't do more. And he knew damn well he wasn't her future.

She released the last button, stripping off his dress shirt. Her eyes followed every movement until it fell to the floor. She reached for his undershirt, slowly drawing it up. Having her blindfolded, reliant on touch, had worked for him last night. But the way her eyes widened as she stripped away his clothes, the way she looked at him as if every inch of his bare skin turned her on, that worked for him, too.

They didn't have much time, though.

Taking over, he pulled the shirt over his head. "Take off your jacket," he said.

She raised an eyebrow, heat flaring in her eyes, but she obeyed.

"Your pants," she demanded.

He unbuttoned the top of his slacks and paused. "Unzip your dress and I'll keep going."

Their game turned into a race, clothes falling to the floor, followed by Amy's hairpins, leaving her long locks flowing freely over her shoulders. Stepping out of his underwear, he reached for her, wanting to strip off her bra, stockings and panties. But she evaded him, sinking down to her knees.

"Amy—"

"Don't stop me, Mark. Please."

Her hand wrapped around his cock, guiding the head to her parted lips. And he couldn't find the words. The sound of the crowd, the dogs barking—it all faded into the distance. Her tongue swirled around the tip, teasing him, as her hand stroked up and down.

Mark closed his eyes, struggling to hold back as she took him into her mouth. And, hell, the way her tongue pressed against him…

Opening his eyes, he stared down at her lips moving over him and groaned.

"Amy, you have to stop," he said. "I'm going to come."

Mark waited for her to pull back. Instead, she pressed her tongue against him, running it up and down until he couldn't hold back. His hips bucked, and his head fell back, his eyes shut tight as the orgasm ripped through him.

When the pleasure subsided, he reached out and ran his hand through her hair before lifting her to her feet.

She looked up at him, her lips forming a devilish smile, and then moved away as if she thought this was over. Not a chance.

"We're not done yet." He gently turned around and had her place her hands on the metal table.

Mark moved behind her, running his hand up the back of her thigh. She widened her stance, arching her back, offering him access. His fingers slipped under her lace panties.

"You're wet," he murmured. He glanced at his discarded pants. He needed to get the condom out of his wallet. He'd slipped it in there this morning just in case they ended up naked again. But that could wait. First, he wanted to touch her, taste her…

He slipped a finger inside as his thumb stroked her. Amy moaned, her hips rocking against his hand. He added a second finger, and her movements turned frantic, hips bucking as she grew closer and closer. Wrapping his hand around her hips, he held her steady.

"Mark, oh, God, Mark." Her fingers pressed into the metal surface. She tossed her head back, eyes closed. "Yes, oh…"

She came hard against his hand, her body trembling. She was far and away the sexiest sight he'd ever witnessed. She took his breath away. She made him want—

"I'm getting a condom," he said. "Don't move."

It took him only a moment to cover himself before he returned to her.

"I want to give you soft and gentle. But…after watching you come, and hearing you scream my name—" he ran one hand up the curve of her back "—I don't think I can hold back. This may be a little rough."

"Yes," she pleaded.

He positioned himself and entered her with one

thrust. Holding her hips, he pushed deeper, took more, needing to drive them both closer to release—

"Amy?" Her cousin's voice drifted through the door followed by a knock. "Are you in there?"

14

AMY GLANCED OVER her shoulder at the solid wooden door as need radiated from her core. As much as she wanted to stay here with Mark, to feel him come inside her, she couldn't. Not anymore.

"Amy?" Eloise called a second time.

Mark withdrew from her and stepped away. She instantly missed the contact, the feel of his skin against hers…

"I'll be right out," she replied, her voice shaking despite her efforts to sound calm and collected while naked and bent over a metal table. Maybe Eloise wouldn't notice.

"Are you okay?" her cousin asked through the door.

"I just needed a break," she called back, standing up and looking at Mark, hoping he would remain silent. It was one thing to be caught hiding from her party alone. But with Mark? She wasn't ready to tell anyone, not even Eloise.

They weren't doing anything wrong. She knew that, but she feared the others wouldn't see it that way.

"I'll be right out," Amy added as she scrambled to

pull on her clothes, wishing she hadn't tossed them in different directions in her haste to undress.

Mark put his pants on before silently turning to help zip up her dress. As she slipped into her blazer and heels, he gathered the rest of his clothes and moved to the far wall, out of sight for when she opened the door.

But he caught her arm as she reached for the handle and leaned close enough to whisper in her ear, "We're not done here. Not even close. Later, when all this is over, I'm going to make you scream with pleasure. Tell me you want that, too."

"Yes."

They'd moved beyond fantasies and rules. She was his, at least for now.

She opened the door and stepped into the corridor. Eloise, wearing a simple black dress that hugged her petite figure, stood with her arms crossed. Her cousin's eyes narrowed as she studied Amy.

"I'm fine, really," Amy said, heading for the whelping room. Eloise might wonder, but maybe the others wouldn't if she brought a puppy out with her to distract from questions.

Eloise followed at her side. "Just taking a break and you managed to lose your pantyhose?"

"They had a run."

"Uh-huh. I always abandon my ruined stockings on the exam room floor, too. What happened to your hairpins? Wait, let me guess, they fell out."

Amy stopped in front of the whelping room and turned to her cousin. "Not another word, Eloise. Please. Not to anyone. If any of the brothers find out…"

"They won't from me." Eloise wrapped her arms

around Amy, hugging her tight. "If he's what you want, I'm happy for you."

Amy closed her eyes. "It's just a fling."

But now that someone else knew, it felt like more.

"Just be careful, Amy. I don't want to see you hurt again."

"Me neither," she said softly.

"And whatever you do, don't fall in love with him." Eloise released her. "That's the first rule. Trust me."

"Said the woman torn apart by Gabe's departure."

"I'll be fine by tomorrow."

Amy squared her shoulders and reached for the doorknob. "Me, too."

"YOU'RE GOING TO HATE ME," Amy said, plopping down on the couch beside Mark, kicking off her heels. She should go upstairs and change. Mark had already swapped his dress clothes for jeans and a long-sleeved blue T-shirt.

Mark raised an eyebrow. "I doubt it. But try me."

"I'm too tired," she continued. "I know it's only our second night, and we were interrupted earlier, but I don't think I have an ounce of energy left."

"Don't be sorry. You had a long, rough day." Mark scooted farther down the couch, away from her, and patted his thigh. "How about a foot rub instead?"

Her eyes widened, and for a moment Amy thought she might cry. "Seriously?"

"Seems only fair since I had the pleasure of watching you walk around in those heels all day."

Amy laughed, shifting on the couch until her bare feet rested on Mark's lap. His large, strong hands went to work kneading her sore muscles.

"I didn't think I'd be in them for so long. But the last dozen or so people simply refused to leave. They wanted tours and to meet the dogs, play with the puppies."

"Can you blame them?" He punctuated the question by running his thumb down the center of her foot, sending a pulse of desire through her tired body. She shifted on the couch as he returned to a deep, intense massage.

"No, I can't. And the Hardwicks offered to adopt Rosie." His hands stilled, but just for a second.

"She isn't cut out for military life," Amy added. "Even home security is questionable. That little girl just loves everybody."

"She raced after the ball alongside her brothers and sisters today," Mark said, and she heard the defensive note in his voice.

"Because she has a crush on you. She wants to be yours." And after the way Mark had helped her through the opening reception, the way he'd made her feel in the vet room, Amy wanted to be his, too.

He pressed his thumb into the sweet spot on her foot again, and this time a moan escaped her lips. Oh, God, his foot massage skills were a bonus.

Rule number three. No one in the military...

No exceptions. Maybe for the puppy, but not for her—at least not in the long-term.

"I can't have a dog," he said. "Where would she live?"

"It wouldn't be fair to take the antithesis of a war dog with you when you deploy," she agreed, only half listening. What he was doing to her feet redefined "foot massage" in her mind. Every touch drew her closer to needing things from him that had nothing to do with caring for sore muscles.

"No," he said, increasing the pressure. "I think the air force frowns on airmen smuggling pets into war zones."

"And you can't just leave her at your home here," she murmured.

His hand stilled. "I don't have a home here. Not anymore. Just a storage unit outside of town for my mom's things, most of which I should probably give away or trash someday soon."

Amy leaned her head back against the couch as his hands started kneading her feet again. He had no reason to come back to Heart's Landing again. Was it intentional on his part? she wondered. Did he want to deploy without a single lasting tie? The thought of him flying out on his missions believing there was no reason to come back made her stomach turn.

A low rumble filled the silence. Or maybe it was hunger pains that had her belly doing somersaults.

Mark's eyes narrowed. "You never ate."

"One broken plate of cookies was enough. Eloise told me they were too good to waste. And there wasn't much left when I came back out."

Mark picked up her feet, set them on the ground and stood. "Put on your shoes. I'm taking you out to dinner."

Amy slipped her tired feet into her heels. "Where are we going?"

"The Last Stop," he said, holding out his hand to pull her up off the couch. "I owe Blanche another visit, and you need a deluxe burger with fries. Maybe a milk shake. Sound good?"

Her stomach answered for her with a second low rumble. "I should change first."

"You look great, Amy." Mark plucked the key to her truck from the table by the door.

"Let's go."

TEN MINUTES LATER, Mark parked her truck in front of The Last Stop Diner and came around to open her door. Holding his hand, she followed him inside. Blanche beamed at them. Amy knew the diner's owner and bumped into her in town now and then, but it had been a while. Blanche looked better than she had in years.

"Wow," Amy said. "I think she is the only part of this place that has changed."

Mark nodded. "Zumba."

Amy stifled a laugh as they approached the counter, claiming two empty stools beside the register.

"Evening," Mark said. "Amy, what would you like?"

"A burger, medium, and fries, please."

"Blanche, add a milk shake. My treat, Amy."

Blanche nodded, scribbling the order on her notepad. "What flavor shake, darling?"

"I really don't need—"

"Chocolate," Mark said. "And I'll have my usual. But hold the salad this time."

"Coming right up." The newly slimmed Blanche marched over to the kitchen window and placed their order.

"Your usual comes with a salad?"

"Blanche's misguided attempts to look out for my health."

The Last Stop's owner returned with two glasses of water. "I heard about your big party. Mrs. Hardwick said it went well. They stopped by on their way home."

"It did," Amy acknowledged, allowing herself to feel

relief for the first time. It was over. No more pretending. She could put the lies and hidden truths behind her—at least some of them. "I think the puppies stole the show."

Blanche shook her head. "I told Mark the other night, I think you're crazy to live out there by yourself with a bunch of attack dogs."

Amy picked up her water glass, raising it to her lips. She'd received countless pats on the back for a job well-done. But no one had called her crazy.

"But I'm glad to see a young woman starting her own business," Blanche continued. "You should join the Heart's Landing Chamber of Commerce."

Amy slowly set her glass back on the counter before she accidentally dumped it in her lap. *Her business.* Of all the people to recognize that she hadn't founded a charity to worship her husband's memory. She looked at Mark out of the corner of her eye. She suspected he'd brought her here for more than the food.

"It took me a while to join," Blanche said. "After I lost my Henry. We'd always run the diner together, but he belonged to the local business associations. They were all a bunch of old boys' clubs back then. Not so much now. They'd welcome you with open arms."

"I'll think about it."

"You do that." A bell rang in the window separating the kitchen from the rest of the diner. Blanche turned. "I'll get your food."

Amy ate half her burger and most of the fries before asking for a to-go bag. Without the bun, the burger would be a nice treat for Jango.

Blanche cleared their plates and returned, her eyes sparkling. "Now, how about some chocolate cake?"

Amy glanced at the glass display case. One frosted

triple layer cake sat on the shelf, and there were only two slices left. Not that it mattered. She couldn't eat another bite.

"A slice for Amy," Mark said. "I'm good."

Before she could object, Mark stood. "Excuse me for a moment, ladies."

When he was out of earshot, Amy leaned forward. "Blanche, I can't eat another bite."

The older woman ignored her, opening the display case and placing the larger of the two slices on a plate.

"That boy." The older woman shook her head as she set the dessert and two forks in front of Amy. "He's been refusing cake since he was little. Always telling me to give it to one of my paying customers. He'd do his schoolwork, never speaking unless spoken to, never asking for anything and refusing half of what I tried to feed him as if there was always someone more deserving."

Amy stared at the rich chocolate frosting. It was so easy to picture Mark as a child, sitting here waiting for his mother to finish her shift. Yes, he'd spent a lot of nights at Darren's house. But not every night. Before he was old enough to stay home alone, it made sense he'd be here. And he wouldn't want to draw attention or cause a fuss, not Mark.

She was still staring at the layered cake when Mark returned to his stool. "You haven't touched it."

"I need your help," she said, wishing she could wrap her arms around him and hold him tight until he understood that he was every bit as worthy of recognition, of happiness and of having a place in this world as anyone else.

Amy held out a fork. "Please. I can't eat this by myself. And I don't think Blanche will let us leave until we finish."

"You sure?" he said. "You only ate half your burger."

"I'm sure." She dug in, forcing one bite on her full stomach, knowing he wouldn't touch it until she did. The top layer of icing slipped off her fork, falling down to her chest. The creamy blend of sugar and chocolate slid down, resting on the swell of her breast just above her neckline.

She reached for a napkin, but Mark's hand trapped hers. She turned to him and caught him staring at her chest.

"Let me," he said.

His gaze swept the room. Before she could object, he lowered his mouth to her chest, swiftly licking the chocolate buttercream off her skin.

"You taste good," he said, picking up his fork.

"Everything's better with chocolate." Her voice sounded breathless and hungry—but not for cake.

15

FIFTEEN MINUTES LATER, after Mark had polished off the cake and tried to pay for their meal—Blanche had adamantly refused his money—they were back in her truck with Mark behind the wheel. Amy felt as if she would explode. Earlier she'd been too tired for sex, and now she was too full. She remembered how his mouth felt on her skin and...God, she wanted him anyway.

But one more feeling crept up on her, adding to her list of reasons to steer clear of Mark and his mouth. She was scared. The things she'd learned about the friend she'd known her whole life made her realize he deserved more than a no-strings-attached fling. And she couldn't give him that without breaking her rules and risking her heart.

They pulled into the driveway, and Amy climbed out of the truck without waiting for Mark to come around and open the door. "I should let Bullet and Nova out."

"I'll join you." He easily caught up with her and then slowed his pace to match hers. She stumbled, her heels sinking into the grass. Reaching out to stop herself from falling, she grabbed his arm, solid and strong.

"Stupid shoes," she muttered, regaining her balance and withdrawing her hand.

"How about a piggyback ride?"

"No." The heat in his eyes, illuminated by the full moon in the Oregon night sky, was like a warning. "I'll be fine. I managed all day in these heels."

"Just to the door."

Amy looked at the wide expanse of grass between them and the kennel's entrance, part of it covered by her tent. She ran back and forth dozens of times a day. But tonight, in these shoes, the familiar space looked as if it had expanded while they'd been out to eat.

"I'm wearing a dress," she said.

"Now that you mention it, I'm going to insist." Mark stepped in front of her and glanced over his shoulder. "Climb on."

She saw the playful challenge in his brown eyes. That look—it felt new and exciting, so different from the concern that had hovered close to the surface during their video chats or when he'd first arrived home. Her fears, the ones she'd brought home from The Last Stop along with her doggie bag, faded into a whisper.

She hiked her dress up to her thighs. "Are you sure about this? I just ate about ten pounds' worth of diner food."

Including chocolate frosting... Her body hummed with the memory.

His brown eyes focused on the edge of her dress, just barely covering her underwear. "Oh, yeah."

She wrapped her arms around his neck as he bent his knees. As she folded one leg around his waist, she felt his arms slide around to her backside, lifting her the rest of the way.

"Ready?" he asked, his voice low and husky as he hooked an arm under each of her legs.

"Yes." But with her dress riding higher and higher, leaving her pressed against the hard wall of his back in only her panties, she was beginning to change her mind about being too tired or too full for finishing what they'd started earlier. One more night, no promises, aside from the assurance he'd never let her fall…

His powerful body easily carried her down the slope and under the tent to the kennel's front door. Mark stopped and released his hold, allowing her to slide to the ground. Her dress moved higher until it decorated her waist.

"Amy." The way he studied her, his broad chest expanding as he sucked in a breath, she wondered if what he really meant was *mine*.

"The dogs," she said, slowly drawing the hem of her dress down to meet her knees.

Mark exhaled, reaching for the door. "I know."

Leading him inside, Amy tried not to think about the way Mark's touch, his voice, his presence behind her, heated her body, begging her to revisit the veterinary room, strip off her clothes, place her hands flat on the metal table and finish what they'd started. She wanted to step back to that place where she could close her eyes and pretend he was a trustworthy stranger intent on pleasuring her.

But that was just a fantasy. And she was beginning to realize the Mark behind the illusion was so much more.

"I'll check on Bullet and Nova if you look in on the puppies," she said. Mark nodded, heading farther down the corridor. Amy went into Nova's and Bullet's rooms, greeting both dogs with a treat and checking to make sure they had water and their doggy doors to their attached outdoor spaces were open. Moving through the tasks, her mind drifted to Mark—in the exam room, at the diner, licking her clean, his hands on her legs as he carried her, the way he'd stood by her all day…

She finished with the dogs and headed for the exit. Her body was on fire with need and wanting. Closing the kennel door behind her, she spotted him leaning against a tent pole, and she knew that she couldn't walk away. Not from him. Not tonight. She wanted to let him in—to her bed, her life and maybe more.

She held out her hand. "Dance with me?"

"There's no music."

"We'll pretend," she said. "Please."

"I don't dance, Amy."

"We both know that's not true," she teased. She moved closer, invading his space, pressing up against him. "Please, Mark."

His hands moved to her hips, and he began to sway with her, slow-dancing to an imaginary song. There were things she wanted to tell him, and it was easier like this with her cheek pressed against his chest, unable to see his expression. The lights illuminating the kennel and the strings of Christmas lights lining the tent's interior had all been removed.

"You deserve a home, Mark," she said quietly. *And I want it to be here. I want to know you'll come back.*

He stiffened but kept dancing. "I'm deployed six months out of the year. When I'm not overseas, I'm training. What I do, it's a single man's game. I thought we were clear on the rules."

"We are," she said. "But that doesn't change the fact

that you're worthy of a real home. People waiting for you to come back—"

"No." Mark froze, drawing back and looking down at her. "I've seen how easily life can slip away and how damn hard the grief is on people left behind. I refuse to do that to someone I care about. I'm not like Darren and his family. I'm not the golden kid everyone will miss."

Amy stepped back, struck by the forcefulness in his tone. "Appearances can be deceiving."

"Darren was my best friend for years, Amy. I knew him. He was a good man. He—"

"He cheated on me."

Amy looked down at the grass, feeling her heels sinking into the dirt. Part of her wanted the ground to swallow her up for saying those words out loud. But now that she'd spoken up, revealing the truth about her marriage, about the man she'd loved in what was beginning to feel like another life, she couldn't hold back. Not anymore.

"He was away so much," she continued. "Deployed for so long, stationed in California, and I lived here..."

Amy had played through all of the excuses, all the reasons Darren had given her for breaking their marriage vows. But Mark didn't need to hear them. Judging from the wide-eyed fury on his face, the way his fists clenched at his sides, this was one secret she should have kept under lock and key.

16

Mark had spent months wishing his best friend was alive and breathing. He'd wanted to slap him on the back and thank Darren for welcoming him into his family, for the long afternoons spent hiking, for having Mark's back for so many years when it had felt as if there was no one else he could count on.

But right now, he wanted Darren alive and breathing so he could kick his ass for hurting Amy.

Mark worked alongside men who deployed for months on end, some away from their wives far longer than they'd planned. But they remained steadfast and loyal to their loved ones.

"Whatever excuse Darren gave you…" Mark said, struggling to keep his tone even. He didn't want to release his temper, not at Amy. The only person who deserved to feel the full force of his fury was dead and buried. "He was wrong. Distance is not a reason to hurt someone you love."

"I know," Amy said. "And I forgave him a long time ago. I'll never know if our marriage would have survived if he'd come back from that last mission alive. I know I wanted him here fighting with me, for us."

His heart broke for her. She'd told him that day after the funeral that not all of her memories were good, but he never imagined this. He wanted to reach for her, draw her close and hold her tight, but he didn't trust himself. Not yet.

"When did you find out?" he demanded, trying like hell to erase the razor-sharp edge in his voice. But, shit, it took everything he had not to spin around and take a swing at the wall behind him.

"When he came home before the last mission. Darren wanted to put it behind us, and he promised it would never happen again. I like to believe he was right about that. People make mistakes. Even SEALs."

"But you still hate hearing everyone talk about him like he was perfect."

"He wasn't," she said softly. "But I can't tell them that. His mother and his brothers don't need to know. They're already hurting so much. I won't add to their pain."

"I'm glad you told me." He buried his burning fury as he drew her close.

"I wasn't planning to." She went willingly into his arms, but kept her palms flat against his chest as she looked up at him. "But I couldn't stand seeing how you keep everyone at arm's length, refusing to commit to anyone or anyplace because you think you don't deserve it. You're not the little boy sitting at the diner counter waiting for someone better than you to take the last piece of chocolate cake."

Mark closed his eyes. He wanted to tell her she was wrong. But for the first time, doubt rose up. The idea of having someone waiting for him, of coming home to a woman… But he didn't want just any woman. For him, it was Amy. He didn't know how it had happened so fast, but over the past few days his feelings for her had changed.

Their friendship was still there, like a concrete foundation. But desire had sprung up like the four square walls she believed should be a part of his life. And he wanted to keep building, seeing where the future would lead them.

Opening his eyes, looking down at her, he knew it was a pipe dream. She had her rules, and he refused to break them. One man had already hurt her, giving her every reason to hate the job Mark loved. He wouldn't be the second to break her heart.

"I might not be that kid anymore," he said. "But setting up a home, getting a dog, even one that lives with someone else eight to ten months of the year, doesn't change the fact that I'm leaving. First, training on base and then, I'll deploy again."

"I know," she said, looking down at her hands. "I didn't tell you this in order to change things between us."

Mark touched her chin, tipping her face up. "Look at me, Amy. I'm going to make you one promise."

"Mark—"

"Listen. Please," he said. "Our friendship is solid. Nothing changes that. You can tell me anything, okay?"

She nodded.

Mark wrapped his arms around her, sliding one hand up into her hair, drawing her head to rest against his chest. He began to move, shifting his weight from one foot to the other. Amy relaxed, allowing him to lead.

Engulfed in silence, without even a dog's bark to interrupt, they danced.

After what she'd shared with him, he'd only planned to offer comfort. This day had been a whirlwind for her. But the way her thighs brushed back and forth against his, the feel of her hips following his rhythm, left him imagining ways to relieve the pressure of this wild day. And those thoughts left him hard and aching for her.

"Mark?" Her voice was a gentle whisper against his chest.

No way she'd missed the rock-solid evidence that his body wanted to give her a different kind of comfort. "Yeah?"

"I'm not full or tired anymore." She moved seductively against him, leaving no room for doubt about where she wanted to take their dance.

He stepped back, reaching for her wrist. "Amy, are you sure? Tonight there are no blindfolds and no games. Just you and me."

"Yes," she said, her blue eyes staring into his, hot and intent.

Relief hit him hard and fast as his desire surged. He wanted her, but not here under the tent. Without a word, Mark scooped her up, one arm cradling her back and the other supporting her legs. Amy's arms closed around his neck as he started for the house.

He practically double-timed it up the grass slope. Letting her down to open the front door, he took her hand, pulling her through the house to the spare bedroom. Closing the door behind them, leaving Jango and the other pieces of their past outside, he turned to her, searching her face for reservations.

Tonight was not about fulfilling fantasies and helping

her move on with her life. He hadn't brought her here to escape. If she wanted to keep her feet firmly planted in blindfolded games, he'd return her to the dog waiting patiently for her in the hall and take a long, cold shower.

Her lips parted, begging to be kissed. Her blue eyes burned bright—everything about her expression screaming, *Take me now, I dare you.*

"Mark?" The low, throaty sound of her voice went straight to his cock.

He wanted her. He craved a taste of the future that would never be his. It might be torture to walk away afterward, but he would. But first, he needed one more night in her arms.

He closed the distance between them, pushing her blazer off her shoulders before turning her gently so that her back was to him. He reached for her zipper, and slowly drew it down her back. Moving his hands over her soft, smooth skin, he guided the fabric down her body until the dress fell away.

He released the hooks securing her bra and reached around her, running his palms over her nipples before cupping her breasts in his hands. Then he turned her to face him.

"Mark, please."

The sound of his name on her lips, the frank acknowledgment that she wanted this, that she wanted *him,* cut through his restraint. He reached for her, kissing her hard. His hands moved to her silky thong underwear, and he pulled them down quickly, eager to see all of her. But he wasn't the only one frantic to remove the barriers between them. Amy stripped away his clothes, kissing him back as if she wished to lead their primal dance.

She pressed her naked body against his, arching her

back until the tight peaks of her nipples brushed his chest. He was heartbeats away from taking her right there in the middle of the room. Amy rose up on her tiptoes, her arms banding tight around his neck. Her right leg hooked around his waist as her hips rocked into him. His mind switched into countdown mode—five, four, three, two—

"Ah, hell," he said roughly. "I need a condom."

"Now," she demanded, releasing him.

Mark scrambled to his rucksack and located the foil packet. He moved quickly as if he'd left a live bomb ready to detonate in the middle of the room. Tearing it open, he covered himself and turned back to Amy. Their eyes locked briefly before her gaze swept over him, the rise and fall of her chest ticked up a notch.

"I like being able to see you," she said.

Her words drove home the fact that she wanted him, not a faceless escape. And he couldn't hold back. Mark closed the space between them and lifted her up, guiding her legs until they wrapped around his hips. With one palm on each cheek, he raised her higher. Then he lowered her down, entering her slowly.

Amy's hands gripped his upper arms, her gaze moving over his muscles. Her tongue touched her lower lip, and he felt the inner walls of her hot, wet core tighten around him. The way she looked at him, as if every inch of his body turned her on, left him struggling to hold back.

He should carry her to the bed. But it was too far. He wouldn't last, not with her thighs squeezing his hips as she raised and lowered herself.

"Amy," he growled.

She looked up, her eyes wild and fierce. This was

a woman who knew what she wanted, who claimed it. Knowing that right now she wanted him, that she had chosen him—something inside him snapped.

Mark captured her mouth, kissing her hard and deep as he carried her to the door. Supporting her against the wooden surface, he drew back, needing to see her as he drove into her over and over.

"Look at me," he said.

Her nails dug into his arms, tempering the overwhelming pleasure rocketing through his body with the slightest hint of pain. Her legs held tight, but she no longer fought to control the motions, letting him take over as he pushed her closer to the brink.

He felt the moment her body tightened around him. He saw it in her eyes. She let out a low moan, a sound he knew would be burned into his memory.

"Come with me," she said.

His jaw clenched as the first spasm shook him, his body ready and willing to follow her orders. He kept his eyes open, letting her watch as the sensations ripped through him. Emotions followed as if surfing the waves of his orgasm, leaving behind words and desires that did not belong in this moment.

Mine. Don't let her go.

Mark rested his forehead against the door, closing his eyes. He'd meant to do this right, to lay her down on the bed and make love to her. Amy ought to be cherished, not taken up against the door in a frantic mating. This should have been about her, damn it. He knew she'd come, but that wasn't enough.

"I'm sorry," he said, slowly stepping back, holding his breath as he waited for her to pick up her clothes and run away again. After the way he'd given in to his desires, he deserved to be left alone to battle his need to keep her.

"For what?" she asked, her voice still breathless as if she was just now finding her way back to reality.

"I didn't mean for it to be like this."

She took his hand, leading him past the pile of clothes on the floor, to the bed. Releasing him, she lay down on her side, one elbow bent with her head resting in her palm.

"If you think you can do better," she said, her voice filled with a sensual promise. "Show me."

17

AMY PATTED THE MATTRESS with her free hand as her challenge hung in the air between them. Stretching her legs, allowing her thighs to rub together, she drew his gaze to the parts of her that begged for more. She couldn't imagine anything better than the feel of his powerful body pushing into her with her back up against the door. His lovemaking had felt urgent and necessary, as if waiting would deplete them both of what they needed.

But then he'd apologized while she was lost in the aftershocks of an orgasm. The parts of her still reeling from pure pleasure begged to know what he'd envisioned for tonight. Right now, she'd willingly follow him anywhere. He could tie her up, blindfold her, whatever turned him on.

When she'd set out to redefine her life, she'd never imagined she would end up here. He had awoken something inside her, leaving her blissfully uninhibited. The shy girl who'd waited, watching her life slip by—that girl was gone.

Amy rolled onto her back, running her hands over her breasts, teasing her nipples. She heard his sharp inhale.

"Mark," she said, turning her head to look at him, noting how quickly his body was recovering from their first round. "Come here."

Jaw tight, he nodded, turning first to his bag and withdrawing a second condom. But instead of rolling it on, he set it beside her on the bed and climbed up, straddling her hips. Gently, he drew her hands away from her breasts and covered them with his own.

He stared down at her, studying her. Amy knew his face. She had spent years reading his expressions. But this look, lust tempered with something more, was new and unfamiliar.

Amy held her breath as Mark leaned forward, lowering his lips to her neck. He trailed kisses over her skin, swirling his tongue, driving her to arch up and press the hard points of her nipples into his hands. He nipped her earlobe, and she moaned, a soft throaty sound she couldn't control.

"Amelia Mae." His rough, low voice left her reaching for him, needing to touch. "I'm going to worship every inch of your body. I am going to feel you come against my mouth, my hands, and then with your tight heat wrapped around me."

"Yes," she pleaded, closing her eyes.

In the back of her mind, that one word—*worship*—echoed. Make love to her, deliver orgasms in sweet succession—yes. She did not want adoration, not from Mark.

His mouth claimed hers, kissing her deeply. His fingers pinched her nipples as his hips lowered to hers. He rubbed against her without slipping inside, and that word drifted away.

"Yes, please, Mark," she said. "Show me."

HOURS LATER, AFTER he'd fulfilled his promise, bringing her to one orgasm after another, he fell back onto the sheets, breathing hard. Amy smiled down at him, her body still humming with mind-blowing pleasure as her mind moved away from a solitary focus on words like *yes*, *more* and *Mark* to the one that hovered over them like a rain cloud. *Leaving.*

It was time for her to go, return to her own bed, before she woke up in the morning with regrets. Sitting up, she moved to the edge of the bed, her feet touching the bare floor.

"Amy, don't go." He reached for her hand, interlaced their fingers. "Let me hold you."

Slowly, knowing she was perilously close to breaking rule four—no strings and no promises—she slid beneath the sheets. Mark pulled her close, wrapping his arms around her as if he worried she might bolt if he let her go.

"I'll stay, Mark," she said, resting her head on his chest. "I'll stay."

In the back of her mind, she knew she wasn't the one who needed to say those words. But she could revisit that thought in the morning, maybe find another loophole. Right now, Mark was here with her, safe in bed, holding her tight.

AMY STARED AT the guest room ceiling listening to the unfamiliar sound of a man snoring softly beside her as sunlight peeked in through the bedroom windows. Add in the fact that his arm rested across her middle, his hand covering her breast as if even in sleep he couldn't stop touching her, and her world felt as if it had rotated one hundred and eighty degrees. Her stomach rumbled, punctuating the thought.

Carefully, she slid out of bed and headed for the door. In the hall, Jango fell in step beside her, his head nudging her hand. She led the dog to the back door without offering excuses for leaving him on the other side last night. She'd taken something for herself and given everything she had to offer, in bed at least, in return. She refused to feel guilty. She opened the door, and Jango dutifully trotted out. Turning back to the kitchen, Amy headed for the coffeemaker.

Strong arms wrapped around her waist as she poured in the water, drawing her back against a wall of muscle.

"Good morning," Mark said.

Amy smiled. "Hi, sorry to sneak out, but I was hungry."

Mark released her, turning to the fridge and opening the door. "I heard you leave, sweetheart," he said, his tone light and teasing.

Amy fumbled the coffee filters, spilling the box on the counter. But Mark scanned the empty shelves, seemingly unaware. Gathering the scattered filters, she placed one in the coffeemaker, focusing on her task, not the surprise at hearing endearments from her friend.

She'd woken wondering if Mark would struggle with the secret she'd shared last night. Would it haunt him, hanging over them like a cloud?

But the day felt new and fresh. He'd teased her, calling her sweetheart. If he was struggling, he was hiding it well.

Mark closed the fridge and turned to her, holding out a paper plate covered in plastic wrap. "It's leftover mini quiche and cookies or nothing."

Amy laughed, leaning toward him, brushing her lips across his as she took the plate from his hands. "Perfect."

Mark followed her to the table and sat beside her. "What's on your list for today?"

"I think you boys have earned a break." She selected a jam-drop cookie. "This is your vacation, after all."

Mark took her hand and squeezed. "I'd rather spend my downtime with you, than kicking around this town."

"Great." Amy glanced at their joined hands. "I know one little puppy who will be happy to see you."

Today was her new beginning. She had to hold tight to that thought. And Mark wasn't leaving. Not today, and probably not tonight.

MARK FOLLOWED AMY, cradling Rosie in his arms. The other puppies raced ahead into the fenced-in area containing the obstacle course, but Rosie seemed content to snuggle close, occasionally lifting her nose to lick his chin.

Amy stopped in front of the kiddie pool filled with plastic balls. Foxtrot glanced back at them as if asking for permission.

"Dive in," Amy said as she turned and took Rosie from his arms. Her hands brushed his chest. The casual touch felt intimate after last night. He'd caressed every inch of her body, learning the places that sparked her desire.

"Sorry, girl," Amy said. "But you can't spend all day in his arms."

But you could. His jaw tightened as Amy bent over and set the reluctant pup in the pool alongside her brothers and sisters. He resisted the urge to wrap his hands around her waist and press up against her. He couldn't. Not out here in the open. But in the veterinary exam room?

His cock stirred, picturing the way she'd looked yesterday, her hands flat on the metal table. He'd told himself last night was enough. But seeing her smiling, devouring cookies with her coffee, had left him wanting more, another night to make love to her and fall asleep holding her close.

"We could let them explore. They won't drown without water in the pool." He moved behind her, his hands giving in to the urge to grab her hips, allowing her to feel how she turned him on.

She leaned her head back against his shoulder. "Can you hold that thought until the end of the morning training session?"

"How long do you plan to keep them out here?" He nipped at her earlobe, needing a taste. "Might get a little uncomfortable."

"Hmm," she murmured, rocking her backside against him. Releasing her right hip, he ran his hand over her jeans, down between her legs, pressing the heal of his hand against the place he'd licked and sucked last night.

"If we wait too long, I might strip you down out here."

"I'm not that wild," she said, stealing glances at the puppies, who were actively exploring the obstacle course.

"Yes, Amy. You are. You're wild and fun." She turned in his arms, mirroring his movements as she wrapped one hand around his hard length through his pants. Mark closed his eyes.

"And I want to play," he added, his voice a low growl of need.

"A game?"

He opened his eyes, his lips forming a wicked smile. "I'm going to count to ten, and then I'm going to find you. And when I do…"

Amy laughed, breaking free from his arms. "You'd better start counting. And no peeking!"

Mark obeyed, ticking off the numbers as he listened for movement. He had years of search-and-rescue training. He could find one woman when the prize was a helluva lot more exciting.

"Ten," he called, opening his eyes and scanning the fenced-in area. "Ready or not, here I come."

He swore he heard the words *oh, I'm ready*, coming from the far left corner of the obstacle course. The tunnel. Mark jogged over, peered inside and found Amy.

He extended his hand to draw her out. "Wasn't much of a challenge."

"Hmm, maybe not." Her hands moved over his chest as she stepped into his embrace. "But I wanted to get to the 'here I come' part."

"Oh, yeah?" Mark wrapped his hands around her hips. "As the winner, I deserve a reward."

Her blue eyes flashed with sensual promise. "What did you have in mind?"

"I want your shirt." He stepped away, placing his hands on his hips, waiting for her to strip it off.

She slowly raised the fabric inch by inch, revealing her smooth stomach, the edge of her lace bra. Drawing the T-shirt over her head, she tossed it aside. A second later, Mark had her in his arms, his hand running over the lace, touching and teasing her breasts. His lips found hers, kissing her deeply.

"Amy?"

He felt her tense at the sound of Luke's voice and

broke away. Stumbling back, her eyes wide, she looked past him. The door leading to the kennel slammed.

"Maybe they didn't see," she said, confirming that both Benton brothers were headed their way.

"Amy." His voice remained calm despite the waves of guilt crashing down on him, one after another. She was topless in a field because of him, dammit. "We're not that far from the door."

And they're soldiers. Nothing wrong with their vision.

Mark turned to face the two men marching toward them, careful to keep Amy hidden behind him. He kept his gaze on the brothers as he tugged his T-shirt over his head and handed it back to Amy.

With Luke and T.J. only a few feet away, Mark widened his stance, bracing for a hit. He stood a few inches taller than the brothers, but it would still be two against one. And Mark didn't plan to fight back. Shit, if he'd caught a man touching Amy, he'd do the same. But for different reasons.

Barking, high-pitched and fierce, diverted his attention from the approaching men. He glanced sideways, watching as Rosie raced in front of him. She stopped short of clamping her jaw around Luke's or T.J.'s ankles, but refused to let them closer. Foxtrot and Charlie followed, ready to join in the fun. The Benton brothers halted, both knowing better than to challenge the pups.

Amy issued a sharp command, but the puppies ignored her. Bending down, Mark quickly gathered Rosie into his arms.

"Calm down, girl," he said. Luke stared at him as if debating whether he was trying to use the puppy as a shield. Once Mark felt the dog relax, he set her down at his feet. "Stay."

Arms crossed in front of his chest, he stood to face the brothers.

"Mind telling me what that was?" Luke demanded. His carefree, smiling veneer had vanished, replaced with a cold, hard glare. The threat of a fist to the jaw alive and present in his tone.

"It looks like someone has a hard time keeping her clothes on around Mark," T.J. added, sliding his hands into his pockets.

"None of your business." Amy moved to Mark's side, his T-shirt hanging down to her thighs.

Luke and T.J. ignored her, focusing on Mark.

"When you said there were guys in town getting ideas that Amy might be available," T.J. said mildly, "you failed to mention you were one of them."

"I didn't want to be." Mark didn't owe these men an explanation, but they needed to understand that what had happened here was mutual. "But—"

"I am available," Amy cut in, taking a step toward her angry brothers-in-law.

"Not to him you're not." Luke's gaze never shifted away from Mark as he raised a finger and pointed at his chest. "I can't believe you. He was your best friend. And here you are, like a mutt searching for scraps."

Fury rushed to the surface. Mark raised his fist. Amy was not a scrap. The beautiful, brave woman standing beside him was not something to be set aside and discarded. First, Darren had acted as if the gift of having her in his life, loving him, wasn't worth damn near everything. And now Luke Benton stood before him suggesting that she was someone else's leftovers. Mark couldn't fight a dead man, but his brother?

Oh, hell, yeah.

"No, Mark." Amy wrapped her hands around his biceps. "Don't. Please. If that is what they see when they look at you, they're blind."

"Amy, it's okay. I know who I am," Mark said. He was still the outsider, the kid with less than everyone else. But these past few days with Amy had shown him that being the "mutt" wasn't so bad.

"But does she?" T.J. challenged. Unlike his brother, the youngest Benton didn't sound hell-bent on proving that Amy still belonged to Darren. There was honest-to-God concern in his voice. "You're leaving, man."

Those words hit home. Mark lowered his hand, gently trying to shake off Amy's hold, knowing he didn't want her close. Not for this.

"You can let go," he said tersely.

"Mark," she said. "This doesn't concern them."

But he shook free from her hold. He stepped over Rosie, stopping within arm's reach of the brothers. He deserved to get the shit kicked out of him because when it came down to it, he wasn't any better than his friend. He'd never hurt Amy the way Darren had. He would never ask for her trust while he put himself in harm's way and then use the distance as an excuse to mess around behind her back. No, he was too damn afraid to commit to her in the first place.

He'd told himself over and over it was because he didn't want to leave someone behind if he lost his life doing his job. But coming home, taking a long hard look at the child he'd been and the man he'd become, he realized he'd offered excuses, same as Darren. He'd told himself it was better for everyone if he breezed in and out of her life—better if he stuck to her rules.

But if another man did that to Amy? He'd start throwing punches. Some rules were meant to be broken.

"Go ahead, Luke," he said. "Take a hit."

18

"ARE YOU CRAZY?" Amy rushed in front of Mark. If the Benton brothers wanted to take a swing, they had to get through her first.

She ignored him, focusing on T.J. and Luke. "Who I date is none of your business."

"She's got a point, bro," T.J. said, rocking back on his heels. "Time to stand down. Both of you."

Luke took a step back, shaking his head. "Ames, you deserve more than a quick fling. And that's all this is, right? A fling?"

The men fell silent, their bodies still poised for battle, waiting for her answer. She'd made love to Mark blindfolded, lost in fantasy. But beyond the bedroom, he'd opened up to her. And she'd trusted him with her secrets. Any other man could walk in and out of her life, but not Mark. She needed him in ways that had nothing to do with sex.

Was this a fling?

No! Yes! It had to be.

A few nights. Nothing more. She'd written rules. It

was her turn to decide what she wanted out of life and go after it, damn it.

"It's none of your concern, Luke," she said, hearing the slight waver in her voice.

She felt Mark's presence, solid like a wall, ready and willing to offer her support. He leaned close, whispering in her ear, "Let's go inside, Amy."

Amy's hand reached for Jango and came up empty. There was nothing at her right side but air. She'd left her dog inside, away from the puppies while they focused on training.

"Please, Amy," Mark said.

She nodded. "Gather the dogs by the tunnel for me?"

"Of course."

Out of the corner of her eye, she saw Mark move toward the puppies. In front of her, Luke spun on his heels, heading for the kennel. She moved to follow him, and T.J. grabbed her arm.

"Wait up, Ames," T.J. said, falling in step at her side.

"I don't want to talk about it, T.J.," she said. "I'm embarrassed enough as it is."

"Don't be. Hell, I'm happy for you. And to be honest, not that surprised. I've seen the way Mark looks at you. But are you sure you know what you're doing? He's heading out. Sooner than you think."

T.J. drew her to a stop. "Amy, I don't want to see you hurt. You're family. I've known you since I was in the seventh grade. You're like the sister I never had. I know I don't have a say in who you date, but I don't want to see you lose another man you care for."

"I won't," she said, but inside she knew it was possible. Her rules wouldn't keep Mark alive when he deployed. And she suspected they wouldn't stop her from caring for him, missing him when he left.

Panic rose and she wanted to run from it, the same way she'd dashed out of her husband's burial. Why was it so damn hard to escape feeling trapped, boxed in by her life and the people around her?

"I need to go," she said, pulling her arm free. "I'm sorry you found out like this. Believe me. But I would appreciate it if you would keep this between us."

"Hell, you think I want to be the one to tell Mom?" T.J. said, his eyes widening.

"There's no reason to tell her," she said quickly. "You're right. This won't last."

Mark returned from the nearby training area and moved to her side. In his hands he held her discarded shirt. "No one is going to tell Mrs. Benton," he said, his voice firm. "Amy was just looking for a way to blow off a little steam. Nothing more."

Amy heard those words and knew she'd hurt Mark. That had never been her intention. Never. She'd been so selfish. She'd wanted to move on, wanted sex—and she'd wanted him. But Mark wasn't a "nothing more." He'd spent too long living by that definition, believing others deserved more than him—especially here in Heart's Landing.

Mark turned to her, offering a reassuring smile. Her stomach churned, and Amy worried she might toss the cookies she'd eaten for breakfast. She should be the one soothing him with plans to write a new set of rules.

Foxtrot sat on her foot. One glance at her most promising dog and Amy knew she couldn't do it. This place, these animals, were her future. The rules stood, no amendments and no changes. She bent over and scooped up the puppy. "I need to go."

Moving quickly, cradling Foxtrot against her chest, Amy headed for the door to the kennel. Inside, she turned to Mark. T.J. followed behind, holding the door for the last of the dogs.

"I'll be back," she said, setting Foxtrot down. "I need to drop by Eloise's place."

Mark caught her arm. "I'm sorry, Amy. I should have known they'd come looking for us."

"Don't apologize," she said, her hand on the doorknob. He'd defended her and helped her keep her emotions in check, forming a buffer between her and the Benton brothers. Without Mark, she might have spilled her secrets.

She glanced over his shoulder at T.J., who remained on the far side of the room giving them space. "You saved me out there," she added.

Mark's hand fell to his side, releasing her. "Most of the time when people tell me that, I'm in a helicopter above a war zone."

"There are different types of saving."

"I know."

"You've been saving me, helping me pick up the pieces, for the past year and a half," she said. "Thank you."

Mark raised his hand to the back of his neck. "You don't have to thank me, Amy. You helped me right back. The past few days have been great…fun."

Amy nodded, knowing there was so much more to the time they'd spent together. She had a feeling he did, too.

TWENTY MINUTES LATER, she walked into Eloise's office. Daisy, the gray-and-white office cat who looked as though she could give the best guard dog a run for his money, greeted her with a suspicious swish of her tail. Only a cat could manage a look that said, *I know you, but I'm still not sure I trust you.*

"I know you're not the only one in the office, Daisy."

"I'm back here," her cousin called from an exam room.

Amy walked past the reception desk and down the hall with Daisy at her heels. Standing in the open doorway, Amy scanned exam room one. File folders covered the metal table. No sign of a four-legged patient. "Pressing paperwork?"

Eloise shrugged. "I need to catch up. I have a busy day tomorrow."

"Uh-huh." Amy didn't buy that excuse for a minute.

"What are you doing here?" Eloise asked without looking up. "Everything okay with your dogs?"

"They're fine." Amy walked into the room and sat down in the blue plastic chair in the corner. "The morning training session went south, but for me, not the dogs. Luke and T.J. caught me fooling around with Mark."

Her cousin glanced up, eyebrows raised. "Look who's wild now."

"Yes. And it felt so good at first." Daisy jumped into her lap, and Amy began petting her. "But now I've made a mess of everything."

"Luke and T.J. will get over it."

"I know, but I told them it was a fling. In front of Mark."

"I thought you two were on the same page."

"We are. But, Eloise, he shouldn't be someone's secret. Mark should have a home with a woman willing to make the necessary sacrifices to become a military wife." She held tight to Daisy, petting her, seeking comfort in the cat's low and steady purr. "And that's not me. I can't do it again. I thought about what a long-term relationship would look like between us, and it would put me right back where I started. Waiting and afraid."

"I wouldn't be so sure about that." Eloise closed the open file folder and set it aside. "You're not the same person you were when you met and married Darren."

"Older and wiser, and look where it landed me. In bed with an airman. I tried writing my own rules. I tried to follow your lead, and I failed. And I'm afraid I hurt Mark in the process."

"You fell in love with him."

Amy let out a laugh. "No, I'm pretty sure there is a firm barrier between selfishness and love. I'm solidly on the self-serving side right now."

"What if you stayed there for a little longer and thought about what you want, not what Mark deserves?" Eloise challenged.

"I can't," Amy said. "There's no room for selfish wants and needs in a relationship with a military man. One thing I learned while married—you love the man, but he's a solider first. His duty to his country comes before your relationship, before everything else in your lives.

"I've finally built a life for myself," she continued. "I don't want to give it up. I need to end things with Mark and move on."

Eloise nodded. "Sounds like a good plan."

"But he's only here a few more days. " Amy closed her eyes. "See, I'm being selfish again, wanting him, even though I know it will be harder on both of us when he leaves."

"I bet Mark likes this selfish side of you. In my experience, a man does not follow a woman into an exam room and strip off her stockings out of the goodness of his heart." Eloise reached for another file folder. "This might sound like a silly question because you have obviously thought this through, but have you even asked him if he wants more?"

"I... You're right." She stood, setting Daisy on the floor. "I need to go back and talk to him."

"Take some gluten-free dog treats with you," Eloise called after her as she headed down the hall. "So you can at least pretend you didn't come here only for my relationship advice."

Amy grabbed a bag from the reception area display shelf and headed for her truck, pausing when she opened the door. Was she making a mistake taking advice from a woman who spent her Sunday doing paperwork instead of dealing with her own feelings? Would talking to Mark change anything?

Probably not. But she owed him a conversation even if it ended with goodbye.

19

"Don't look at me like that."

Jango sat on his bed in the corner of Amy's kitchen, watching as Mark searched for a pad of paper and a pen. Finding what he needed, Mark wrote a quick note for Amy and set it on the table.

"I'll be back in a few hours," he said to the suspicious dog. "It's your job to make sure she sees that note. I don't want her thinking I got spooked after this morning and ran away."

He was running, but it wasn't away from her. He was barreling headfirst past the barrier erected by her rules, bypassing words like *fun*, and rushing straight for a word he had shied away from for as long as he could remember—*commitment.*

Mark tapped the piece of paper on the table. Jango lay down on his bed, his gaze fixed on the note. If there was one thing this dog loved, it was a mission.

"Sometimes I think you understand everything we say," Mark muttered as he went to the front door.

Outside, T.J. stood beside his mother's compact sedan. Mark headed over, wondering if this was a bad idea. Maybe he should wait here and talk to Amy when she returned. To hell with the grand gestures.

"Thanks for coming," Mark said when he reached the passenger-side door. "I'd go myself, but I need your wheels and your expertise."

"No hard feelings, man." T.J. slid into the driver's seat and started the engine. "Not from me. Luke? Well, he's another matter."

Mark nodded. Luke's feelings didn't concern him. Right now, Amy was all that mattered.

They drove in silence past Heart's Landing's familiar landmarks, including The Last Stop Diner. Beyond the town limits, the landscape turned to trees and farms.

"Mind telling me why you're hell-bent on making this trip today?" T.J. asked.

"I want to do something for Amy." Mark focused on the tall pines outside the window. "Show her that I care."

T.J. steered the car onto the four-lane highway. "Most women like flowers, chocolate, a night out at a place where they charge you five times what the food is worth."

Shit, he didn't know the first thing about flowers and chocolate. He doubted Amy wanted to leave her dogs behind for a night out in Portland, where the restaurants fit T.J.'s description. "Amy's not most women."

T.J. nodded. "She's special. I'll give you that, but I still think flowers might be the way to go."

Doubt hung over his head. Was he making a mistake dragging T.J. out for a three-hour round-trip shopping adventure when Amy would rather have a dozen roses?

"I want to leave her with something she can use," Mark said. "Something that will keep her safe."

"You're the one who's trying to win the girl." T.J. took

an exit. "Check the directions. I haven't been to this place in years, and I want to make sure we don't get lost on back roads in the middle of nowhere."

"I'm not trying to win her. Amy is not a prize. I just want her to know she means something to me." Mark scrolled through the directions on his phone. "Turn right at the next light."

A while later, they pulled up to the store. Mark had called ahead to make sure it would be open on a Sunday afternoon. The lights were on, and two cars were parked in the lot.

"Have an idea of what you want?" T.J. asked.

"Whatever will offer her the most protection," Mark said. "And make her smile when she sees it."

T.J. shook his head. "I hope you know what you're doing."

AMY OPENED THE FRONT DOOR and found Jango standing on the other side, tail wagging. She moved out of the way and waited for him to rush past her. But instead he barked and raced to the kitchen.

"Hungry, boy? It's a little early for dinner."

The Belgian Malinois sat beside the kitchen table and barked again. Amy walked over and spotted the note. Her stomach sank. Mark had left. Hurt by her words, he'd decided to cut his ties and return to base. Or worse, he'd been called back.

Helpless dread threatened to overwhelm her. Amy closed her eyes and focused on breathing. Part of her wanted to run away now, escape to her kennel and seek comfort in her dogs.

Jango barked, and she forced herself to open her eyes and pick up the paper, her hands trembling. She'd known from the beginning Mark was leaving. Leaving defined a soldier's life. It was always a matter of time.

Steeling herself, she looked down at the note in her hand.

> Needed to pick something up. Might take a few hours. I'll be back for dinner.
> Mark
> P.S. I tried texting you, but found your phone beside the coffeemaker.

Amy spun around and picked up her cell. She'd been in such a rush to get away and clear her head earlier, she'd forgotten to take it with her. Then she turned back to Jango, who'd moved closer to where she kept his treats.

"Did he really go shopping?" she asked, reaching into the jar and pulling out a biscuit.

Jango's tail thumped against the floor, his eyes tracking her hand. She tossed the treat to him. Catching it, he retreated to his bed.

"I guess I'll find out."

Hours later, after she'd fed and played with her dogs, Amy headed back to the house. Still no sign of Mark. And this time, she'd kept her phone on her. She'd been tempted to call or text, but then thought better of it. He didn't owe her anything.

Elizabeth Benton's car pulled up the driveway, and Amy slowed as she approached the front of her small home. Mark had gone shopping with her former mother-in-law?

"Hi, Ames." T.J. waved from the open driver's-side window, adding another layer of confusion. T.J. hadn't been the one ready to throw punches earlier, but she hadn't expected him to take Mark, or anyone, *shopping*.

"Hey," Mark said as he climbed out and went to the back of the car.

"Hi." Amy tried to put the pieces of this puzzle together in her mind. Had he gone out for groceries, wanting to fill her empty kitchen before shipping out?

Withdrawing a large rectangular box, Mark slammed the trunk closed and headed for the porch. "Thanks again, T.J."

"Anytime." T.J. smiled at her. "Don't blame me if you don't like it. I told him to go with flowers."

Flowers? Why would Mark bring her flowers?

"Ignore him." Mark opened her front door. Amy followed him inside as the sound of the car on her gravel drive faded away.

Carrying the large box as if it was featherlight, Mark led the way into the kitchen. He wore the same green camo-patterned cargo shorts he'd pulled on that morning, but he'd changed into a faded gray air force T-shirt. Amy studied the lettering across his strong, broad chest. It was the first time he'd worn clothing that labeled him a member of the US military since he'd arrived. Was that a sign he was heading back?

"How are you?" He set the box down on the kitchen table. "Did you feed the dogs?"

"Yes," she said, staring at the box that did not contain flowers.

Mark smiled and nudged it toward her. "You can open it, you know."

"You didn't have to get me anything." Her fingers snapped the Scotch tape securing the sides.

"I wanted to."

Amy lifted the top and peered inside. Her eyes widened. Tossing the lid to the floor, she reached for her present. "You got me a compression sleeve?"

"To help with the bite work." Mark shoved his hands into his pockets, rocking back on his heels. Out of the corner of her eye—it was impossible to entirely tear her gaze away from her present—she saw Mark's expression lit with excitement, as if he'd been worried she wouldn't like the gesture.

"I dragged T.J. along, and he said this was the best brand on the market and one of the few with a model made for women." He pointed to the portion designed to protect her upper arm. "This part is solid, but the sleeve has room for movement. There's a handle inside, and… do you want to try it on?"

"Yes." She turned the training tool over in her hands. She'd planned to order one at some point, but there had been so many things to purchase for the kennel that she'd put it off.

Mark moved to her side and waited for her to hand over her gift. She complied, holding out her right arm. He slipped it on, and her hand found the handle inside. The large padded area extending from her forearm formed a triangular point perfect for training a dog to bite. It was big enough to force the pup to open his mouth wide, but also had some give, allowing the animal to hold on.

While Amy turned it, admired the fit, which was perfect for her smaller frame, Mark reached into the box and withdrew two white cloth covers.

"T.J. recommended these. One for the puppies and one for the adult dogs. The thicker one can be too hard for a young dog to hold on to."

She ran her hands over both, feeling the differences in the fabric. "I hadn't thought about that," she admitted.

"So, you like it? Better than roses?"

Looking up at him, something inside her melted. And she had a sinking feeling it was her resolve. His gift spoke directly to who she was and what was important to her. It said *I understand you* in a way that roses never could.

"This is so much better than flowers," she said softly. "But you didn't need to go to all this trouble."

"Facing Luke and T.J., trying to explain what we're doing together, something became clear to me."

Her grip tightened on the protective sleeve. It looked like a piece of armor, a protective barrier against attack. Too bad it didn't cover her heart, because right now that was the most vulnerable part of her body.

"Any man who comes into your life should treasure you. Romance you. You're special, Amelia Mae."

"Mark, please." She needed him to stop before he said too much. "I don't want to be romanced. I just need..."

Mark. But she wanted him here. With her.

He brushed his fingers across her cheek, tucking stray strands of hair behind her ear. "You mean so much to me, Amy. And after what happened earlier, I felt you should know."

His lips touched hers, kissing her softly. She closed her eyes, knowing she should step back. They needed to talk. She had to explain that she couldn't break rule number four.

But then his hands held her head, deepening the kiss. She gave in, taking everything he offered. It was selfish, but she took the kiss, needing his touch.

Hips pressed against him, she felt his thigh vibrate.

It ended and then started again. Reluctantly, he released her, withdrawing his phone and checking the screen.

"I need to take this." Mark moved toward the hall as he offered the person on the other end a curt greeting.

Amy slipped her arm out of the sleeve, gently setting it down in the box. It was the most thoughtful gift anyone had ever given her. How many men would stand up to the Benton brothers, offer her gifts that brought her closer to making her dream for these puppies a reality, and then kiss her senseless? Maybe she was making a big mistake clinging to her rules. Maybe—

"Amy."

She turned around and saw Mark standing in the entryway to the kitchen. The muscles in his jaw were tight. There was no sign of the smiling man who'd driven all over Oregon to buy her a present. This man was determined and tense, every inch a warrior.

"That was my commanding officer. They have asked me to return to base. They need me back in Afghanistan."

20

AMY STEPPED BACK, reaching behind her for the table's edge, needing the hard surface to keep her upright and balanced.

Leaving. Shipping out. For Afghanistan. Now.

The maybes, the what-ifs, they vanished with those words.

"But you just got home," she said, echoing what she'd repeated over and over to another man in what felt like another life.

"I signed up to fill the shortfalls."

"You asked to go back?"

"If they needed me. And they do." There was so much sadness in his brown eyes. "One of our helicopters was hit. Only two PJs survived."

"Oh, God." Those poor men—and their families, probably opening their doors to a person wearing a uniform. Those wives, mothers, fathers and children sitting down and listening as the stranger cut apart their lives with news no one imagines would hurt so damn much.

"Did you know them?" she asked.

"I didn't find out who was in the helicopter," he said. "They haven't notified all of the families."

"Of course." Her body was numb, and it felt as if her world was shifting to autopilot. Jango moved to her side, pressing against her leg. She reached down and touched the top of his head. "When do you leave?"

"In the morning. First thing. I'll see if T.J. or Luke will give me a ride to the airport. I know you need to be here with your dogs."

"I'm sure one of them will."

Mark stepped forward, his brow knitted together. "Amy, I meant what I said before the call. Over the past few days, you've become a part of my life that I don't want to walk away from. I never thought I'd feel that way about anyone. For so long, I thought I was lucky that no one was waiting for me back home. I told myself I wasn't worth the heartache."

Her anger sparked. "Don't you dare say that."

He moved closer, stopping within arm's reach. Amy ran her fingers through Jango's short hair. She refused to give in to the temptation to touch Mark, kiss him and draw him close. He was *leaving*, damn it.

"You're an amazing man, Mark." Her voice wavered as she said his name.

"I'm glad you think so." He offered her a tentative smile. "Because I don't want this to be goodbye. In four months, six months, whenever this tour ends, I want to come back to you. You told me that I deserved a home. I want it to be with you."

Her hand stilled on the top of Jango's head. "You can't promise you'll come back."

His smile disappeared. "No. I can't. But there is a long list of promises that I can make to you. I swear on my mother's grave that I will never break your trust. And you have my word that I will help you follow your dreams. I'll be there for you as a friend and lover. I promise to do my best to stay safe every time a mission drops and my team heads out.

"I'm good at what I do, Amy. If that offers you any comfort, know that I take every precaution when my life and my team's lives are at stake. But we still go in, and we rescue the person who has fallen. Maybe I took on this job because of my childhood, because I wanted to prove I could be so much more than that quiet kid, to show the world that I can help people. I don't know. And in the moment when another man or woman's life depends on me doing my job, it doesn't matter why I'm there."

Part of her wanted to scream, *Yes, I'll wait for you!* But fear rose up like a wild animal threatening to tear her to pieces. Maybe it made her the greediest person on the planet, but she had her calling and he had his. They'd shared so much over the years, growing closer these past few days, becoming lovers… But their work, their passions, were like parallel paths that never intersected.

"Amy?" He ran the back of his hand over her cheek.

"I've finally found a way to move on," she said slowly. "I'm sorry, Mark, but I can't go back. The deployments, the fear, the not knowing…I can't do it again. You should have someone to come home to. But that person isn't me."

"I understand," he said tightly. "You were clear about the rules from the beginning. I just thought… Shit, it doesn't matter what I thought."

"I'm sorry," she repeated, her voice shaking.

His brown eyes studied her as if trying to memorize

every last detail of her face, knowing he wouldn't be coming back. At least, not here.

Amy fought back a sob at the thought of losing him completely. "I have no right to ask," she said. "But will you keep in touch?"

"I'll try." He nodded to the doorway. "I should go. I'll call T.J. and ask for a ride."

He turned to leave, and she reached for him. "Wait. Before you go."

She wrapped her arms around him, hugging him tight, feeling every solid inch of him pressed up against her. This time, the feel of his body offered comfort, not lust. Mark was strong. And he was a fighter. He'd stay safe and come home alive.

Just not to her.

AMY WORE THE COMPRESSION SLEEVE on her arm as she headed back to the kennel. T.J. and Luke walked beside her, leading Foxtrot.

"Not bad for his first lesson," Luke said, offering the puppy another treat. "He got a full grip and didn't let go."

"He's my star." She held the door.

"That sleeve helps." T.J. gave her covered arm a pat as he walked past. "I'm sorry Mark got called back when he did. The man deserved a proper thank you for a gift like that."

"Shut up, T.J.," Luke snapped. "I've come around to the idea of Amy and Mark together, but I don't need a mental picture."

Amy followed the brothers down the hall to the whelping room. "We're not together. It's over. Neither of you need to worry."

She shrugged out of the sleeve while Luke led Foxtrot inside.

"Need help with that?" T.J. asked.

"No," she said, setting it in the hall. "I'll put it away later. Let's head in and check on the others."

"They're probably still exhausted from their morning exercise," T.J. said.

Amy worked alongside the brothers, petting the puppies and checking their water. In a few days, T.J. would return to his work at Lackland, and then a week later, Luke would leave. It would be just her and her dogs, which is exactly what she'd wanted.

"Amy, your personal life is none of my business," T.J. said, kneeling in front of Rosie's cage. The puppy had been moping ever since Mark's departure. "But I noticed he spent the night in Jeremy and Gabe's old room."

"Is this what you do down at Lackland?" Luke demanded. "Gossip like a bunch of girls?"

"When I drove him to the airport this morning, Mark didn't exactly seem happy with the way you left things," T.J. added, ignoring his brother.

Amy's hand froze midair, holding a tennis ball. "Did he say something?"

"Only that he doesn't plan to return to Heart's Landing," T.J. said.

"Ever?" Luke asked.

T.J. stared at her. "Said there was nothing here for him."

Amy looked away, releasing the ball. "He has a storage unit."

"He's planning to have the owner box it up and ship it to him," T.J. replied.

The reality sank in. Mark wasn't coming back to this

town. And why should he? This place held nothing but bad memories for him.

But hearing T.J.'s words and recognizing the truth, it brought her close to tears. Never was a very long time. She'd been so afraid she would lose him on the battlefield, she hadn't stopped to consider that if he simply walked away and never looked back, it would hurt just as much. The reality of never seeing him again, never holding him or hugging him again—it was like a physical wound.

"Amy, honey, I don't know what happened between the two of you," T.J. continued. "But I know for a fact that man cares for you."

"He does," she said, her voice wavering. "But knowing he cares—that is not enough. I can't go back to the life I had."

"Maybe this time would be different," T.J. said. "Mark's not a SEAL."

"It doesn't matter. For me, for the person waiting, his job or which branch of the military he serves in does not matter. When Mark goes out on a mission, his focus will be on saving that life. He'll be 100 percent in the moment. And that soldier, civilian, whoever he saves, will be so fortunate he's there. But if I said yes, if I agreed to wait for Mark, I would spend every day wondering if he's safe. No matter how busy I am, I'll never forget that he could die at any moment. I'll keep going, working, paying the bills, moving through the motions of living, waiting for him to come home. But inside, fear will follow me everywhere.

"I can't risk losing my sense of self, my independence and maybe the man I'm waiting for. You can't possibly understand—"

"But I do." Elizabeth Benton's voice echoed against the whelping room's cinder-block walls. "I know what it is like to be a military spouse and mother."

"Shit," Luke said.

"Watch your language, Lucas." Mrs. Benton walked into the room.

"How much did you overhear?" T.J. asked grimly, his hands on his hips.

"Enough to confirm what I already suspected," she said, smiling up at Amy. "I saw the way Mark looked at you during dinner the other night. And I hoped you two wouldn't let the past hold you back."

"I… We—" Amy searched for the right words. "But it is."

"Boys, why don't you check on the other dogs? Nova and Bullet looked lonely when I walked past their rooms," Mrs. Benton said.

"Yes, Mom," the brothers said in unison, heading for the door.

"I'm so proud of what you've built. I must admit I got a bit caught up in the excitement of the opening. But then, I look for any excuse to demand my boys use their limited vacation time to come home," her former mother-in-law said.

"I appreciate everything you did to make it happen," Amy said quickly. "I want you to know that Mark and I, we didn't plan what happened."

"You can't plan love," she said. "If you could, all those couples on reality TV would end up spending the rest of their lives together. And I think we both know most sensible women would steer clear of a military marriage."

Amy nodded.

"But love isn't sensible. You fall for the man, not his job," Mrs. Benton continued. "And you choose to make it work."

Amy searched the older woman's face, lined with years of worry and heartbreak. "How do you do it? Your sons, all of them, decided to put themselves in harm's way. And after losing a husband...how do you make it through each day not knowing if they're safe and alive?"

Mrs. Benton shrugged. "I trust they are good at their jobs. Sometimes it helps me to remember that people die in everyday life. I know it sounds morbid, but there is always a chance you could lose the people you love to a car crash or illness. And Heaven knows, there were plenty of times when my boys were young, I thought I would lose them to an accident.

"Did you know Luke and Jeremy once jumped out of a tree with towels tied on as capes? They wanted to see if they could be superheroes. Each boy broke a leg."

"I heard the stories," Amy said.

"At least now they have the training to go out into the world and be heroes." Mrs. Benton shook her head at the memory. "My husband and my boys felt called to serve their country. I can't change that, and if I could, I'm not sure I would want to. I love them for who they are."

Amy bit her lip. For weeks, she'd wanted everyone to see past the labels, to understand that she was not Darren's perfect widow. And yet, she'd turned around and done the same to Mark. He was an airman who saved lives. Yes, that might complicate their future together. It might be hard, but he deserved to be loved for who he was.

"Excuse me," she said, moving toward the door. "I need to go win back my hero."

21

MARK CLIMBED INTO the helicopter waiting at the NATO hospital. They'd delivered the patient—a child caught in the cross fire between US military forces and Afghan insurgents—in stable condition. And for the first time in weeks, Mark felt like smiling.

They flew the short distance to their base and headed for the barracks to clean up. Out there, on a mission, he felt alive and sure of himself. He was 100 percent focused on saving the patient. But back at the barracks, his mind wandered, returning to Heart's Landing. He never planned to set foot in the town again, but that didn't magically wipe out his memories.

And, shit, the emails from Amy weren't helping. He'd received the first one, asking to video chat, the day after she booted him out of her life. The sting from her rejection was still there.

"Hey, Mark, what the hell?" Teddy, one of the younger guys on the team, called. "We save a ten-year-old boy's life in front of his weeping mother and you're frowning? You rocked that mission."

"Tired, that's all." He turned away from the rest of

his team, heading for his bed. He had twelve hours before his next shift. He should shower and get to bed. But he knew he'd end up checking his email first. Just because he didn't respond didn't mean he wanted to stop hearing from her. He liked reading about her day and seeing pictures of Rosie—though she'd stopped sending those in an attempt to get him to respond. If he agreed to a video chat, she'd bring the dog.

But he wasn't ready. He needed to bury the hurt a little deeper before he saw her and talked to her again. It might be easy for her to follow the playbook she'd laid out and go back to where they'd been before, but he couldn't do it. Not yet.

Shaking his head, he opened his computer and logged on. And there it was, his daily email from Amy. Only this one didn't mention a video chat or offer a picture of the puppies. This time, she'd written a list.

Dear Mark,
For months, I sent you my memories. And when you came home, I shared my secrets with you. Now I'm mourning a different loss—what we might have had together if only I'd opened my heart and mind to the possibility earlier. I'm sorry. I allowed fear to guide my choices, instead of love.

I'm sorry and I've fallen in love with you. Those are words I wished to say to your face, or at least to your image on the computer screen, but you refused to answer my emails, so I'm writing them here.

I know how we got here, but I can't find my way back. Following your advice, I've made a new list of memories. Below are the moments that brought me to this place...

1) I saw your chest on the computer screen. And I

stared (longer than I should have) at your muscles. At the time, it felt inappropriate. But I'm not sorry.

2) You caught me in my underwear.

3) You saw me for who I wanted to be, not an image or a label. I only wished I'd returned that kindness sooner.

4) We kissed. If you'd like to know more about this memory, well, you'll need to respond to my emails.

5) We danced. I still hear that song in my dreams sometimes. I wake up wanting and I… Again a response is required to learn more.

Love,
Amelia Mae

Mark read the email a second time. Amy was in love with him. How? When? The questions scrambled in his head as his lower half responded to number five. *Amy* and *sex*—again those words wreaked havoc.

He'd been determined to move on, to focus on doing his job. He belonged here, saving lives, not tied to a town that offered nothing more than bad memories.

Except they weren't all bad. He'd kissed Amy for the first time in Heart's Landing. With her by his side, he'd locked the ghosts from his childhood where they belonged—in the past. And he'd fallen in love there.

Mark opened the laptop and began typing.

"DON'T GET YOUR hopes up," Amy said to Jango and Rosie as they sat down on either side of her chair, their eyes focused on the kitchen table.

She'd moved the puppy into the house last week, knowing that continuing her training wouldn't change the fact that she'd never serve in the military or work with a police force. And even if she miraculously showed an interest in learning the necessary skills, Amy didn't want to let her go. Rosie belonged here.

Every morning, she fed the dogs, made her coffee and sat down at the computer to check her email. But fourteen days later, she still hadn't heard from him. She'd convinced Luke to call and pretend the army needed to know if the latest team of PJs had deployed, but they'd refused to give him an answer.

For all she knew, he'd been killed in action. No one had bothered to tell her because they weren't family. But she'd pushed the thought aside. Mark was alive. And she was determined to become his family.

Opening her inbox, she scanned past the junk mail and saw his name.

"He responded!" she cried. Both dogs jumped up and barked, nearly knocking her coffee mug off the table. "Mark sent an email!"

Settling into her chair and trying to appear calm, for the dogs' sakes, she opened the message and started reading out loud.

Dear Amy,

I have so much to say to you, but I'll wait until we talk. My shift starts again in eleven hours, about when you'll be starting your day. But if we have some downtime, I will send you a message and see if you are online. Until then, here is my list:

1) The joy in your bright blue eyes when you first told me about your war dog training and breeding center.

2) The feel of your body pressed against me the night you "sprained" your ankle. (I also thought about fighting T.J. for the right to examine your foot. Not be-

cause I wanted to maintain the ruse. The idea of another man touching you, even your ankle, bothered me.)

3) The way you talked about your vibrator and living in the moment after we caught a glimpse (which I've tried to erase from my memory) of your cousin and Gabe.

4) The way you looked blindfolded, moving to the rhythm, willing to follow my lead.

5) Call me and I'll tell you… If I continue, I'll need a cold shower.

I'll leave you to think about my list. I recommend focusing on number 4, and not just because it might leave you wanting. I want to lead you into a future where the little moments, the memories, matter more than the obstacles in our path.
Mark

"Blindfolded, huh?"

Amy looked up from her computer screen and spotted Eloise, one shoulder leaning against the doorway, her arms crossed in front of her chest. A box of doughnut holes dangled from her fingers.

"I'm not the one who had sex in the Tall Pines Tavern parking lot with my hands tied behind my back," she said, eyeing the box. When was the last time she'd eaten?

Her cousin's face fell, but only for a second. Then she stepped into the kitchen and set the box on the counter. Lowering down to the dogs' level, she greeted Jango and Rosie. "Why don't I take care of the dogs today?"

Amy closed her laptop and pushed back from the table. "You don't have to do that."

"If Mark sent that last night, his shift has probably already started."

"Someone was eavesdropping for a long time."

"That will teach you to read naughty emails out loud to your dogs," Eloise said with a smile. "Now sit down and send him a message so he knows you're ready whenever he is."

"If you insist."

"I do." Eloise pointed to the doughnuts. "And eat. You're too skinny again."

"Okay." Amy grabbed the box and sat, opening the computer screen. "But leave Rosie. Mark will want to see her."

Eloise shook her head and opened the door, releasing the dogs into the yard. "Next time. She's young. And if number four involved a blindfold, I don't think she should hear number five."

"Eloise," she protested. "Mark should see his dog."

Her cousin laughed. "I knew you were saving Rosie for him. Tell him I'm holding her ransom until he agrees to love and worship you forever."

The door closed behind her cousin, leaving Amy alone in the kitchen with her laptop. She quickly sent a one-sentence message to Mark letting him know she was at her computer. Glancing at the coffeepot, she debated another cup. But she was already so nervous.

She'd opened her heart to him in her email. Yet, in his response, he hadn't mentioned love. What if she'd pushed too far, too fast?

Her fingers drummed against the desk. When she'd sat down at her computer this morning, she had expected to find her inbox filled with garbage, not a list from Mark. But now, after two weeks, she was finally going to see his face again. Talk to him. If she'd known, she probably would have taken a shower.

Eyes wide, she jumped up, taking the laptop with her as she headed for the stairs. She needed to wash her face, brush her hair and change into clean clothes. Setting the computer on the bed, she scrambled to the attached bath, quickly splashing water on her face. Stripping out of her clothes as she returned to the room, she opened her drawers and paused.

Feeling Lucky. The red words stared up at her from the top of her underwear pile.

Amy laughed. Yes. Today, she felt lucky and hopeful. Maybe they could make this work. Maybe he loved her back.

She stripped off the boring clothes she'd pulled on this morning when the dogs first woke her and pulled on her lucky underwear. Reaching for her jeans, she heard the ding signaling a new message.

Amy dropped the pants and ran to her computer. It wasn't an email. He'd sent a request to video chat. She clicked the accept button, kneeling down on the floor so that her face was within the camera's scope.

Mark appeared on her screen. He was sitting in what looked like his bedroom, if one could call a bed surrounded by a curtain a room. His uniform shirt stretched tight across his chest. She knew if the call came, he'd strap a vest over it.

"Hi," she said. "Thank you for responding. I was starting to worry about you. Rosie was, too."

He smiled. "How is she? Rosie?"

"Great. She's living in the house now with Jango. Waiting for you."

"Sounds like I have a dog. Guess that means I'll have to come back."

She nodded. "And me. You have me."

"What made you change your mind?" he asked so softly she barely heard the words.

"Elizabeth Benton." Mark's eyes widened, but she kept going, needing him to hear this and worried they'd run out of time. He could be called away at any moment. "She made me realize that I was hiding behind fear. I don't want to be left behind, grieving for another man, but that doesn't change the fact that I've fallen in love with you. And, Mark, you're worth risking my heart. I'm sorry I was too blind to see it before you left. I should never have pushed you away."

"You're forgiven. I should have realized your rules needed to be broken earlier. You and I, we were never a fling."

"I know." Amy rested her elbow on the bed, wanting to be closer to him. She wished she could crawl through the screen and wrap her arms around him. "I wish I could kiss you."

"The curtains closed. You could always show me what happens when you dream about our dance."

"I'm not that wild."

"Sweetheart," he said, smiling. "I've seen you blindfolded."

Amy laughed, leaning closer, accidentally causing the computer to slide down the bed, taking the attached camera with it. She rose to set it back in place.

"Wait," Mark's voice called as she made the adjustments. "Are you wearing your lucky underwear?"

She quickly adjusted the screen to show her face. "I thought I might need a little extra luck."

"What happened to your pants? And don't give me the my-dog-ate-them line. You've used that excuse before."

"I was in a hurry."

"I think you wanted me to read your underwear."

She smiled. "Maybe."

"Stand up," he said. "Let me see."

Leaving the computer perched on the bed, she stood and moved away slowly.

"Sweetheart, you have no idea how sexy you are." His voice was low and rough.

His words, the blatant wanting in his eyes, ignited her daring. She reached for the hem of her T-shirt, drawing it up, revealing her stomach. "Tell me."

Heat flashed in his brown eyes. "The fact that I can't get my hands on you right now—"

"Scramble. Scramble."

The order blasted through the base's PA system, drowning out Mark's voice.

"I have to go." His desire vanished, replaced with cool, calm focus. Reaching out, he touched the screen.

Amy moved closer to the computer, lifting her hand to meet his. "Go. Save a life. I'll be here when you get back."

The raw emotion on his face, as if he'd been waiting for years to hear those words, sent her rocking back on her heels.

"I love you, Amelia Mae." He stood and slowly backed away from the screen.

"I love you, too," she called, holding his gaze for one last moment before he disappeared through the curtain. "I love you, too."

Epilogue

"ARE YOU SURE you can handle this on top of your practice?" Amy asked, tossing an emergency bag of doggy treats into her carry-on.

"If I say no, are you going to cancel your trip?" Eloise challenged. "You haven't seen Mark in six months. If he's going to be stationed at the air force base in New Mexico for a month, maybe more, wouldn't you rather be there, too?"

"You're right. But we could stay a few more days. Mark isn't scheduled to arrive until the end of the week."

"You need to use that time to move into your rental apartment near the base," Eloise pointed out. "Set up your big surprise."

Amy nodded. "We're going. Today. Right, Rosie?"

The dog lifted her head, tail wagging.

Amy picked up Rosie's harness. "While I'm down there, we're going to drive over and visit her brothers and sisters at Lackland. See how their training is going."

After months of training, Rosie's four littermates had been purchased by the military. Her business, her dream, was a success.

Securing the harness, Amy paused, staring at her kennel through the kitchen window. Part of her wanted to be here when Nova and Bullet's second litter was born. But Mark would only be home for a short time. And there would be another litter of puppies once the new female dog—the one Elizabeth Benton had graciously agreed to pick up for her—arrived from Europe. Her mother-in-law intended to visit Paris and London first. Amy was glad to see Elizabeth doing something for herself. Life shouldn't only be about waiting.

Leading Rosie to the door, she gave Jango one final pat on the head and hugged her cousin. "Please, call me if you need help."

Eloise squeezed her tight. "I will. And I won't be alone the whole time. T.J. promised to come up and help if he could get away. If not, he'll send one of his brothers."

Amy laughed. "Because the rest of the Benton boys have so much control over their schedules."

"Either way, we'll be fine," Eloise said. "I don't need a Benton to help look after your dogs."

"Of course you don't. I should go. I don't want to miss the flight and start all over convincing the airline to give Rosie a seat. The woman I spoke with this time was so eager to help, she upgraded both of us to first class."

"Now you're just making me jealous." Her cousin gave her a playful push. "Go."

Amy led an eager Rosie to the truck. "You know we're going to see Mark, don't you?"

The dog gave a series of sharp, happy barks and then hopped into the passenger seat without a backward glance. Amy went around to the other side and did the same. It was a lot to leave behind—her kennel and her dogs—but she had help, and she'd be back soon.

Right now, she needed to give Mark a proper homecoming.

DIRTY AND TIRED after the long flight from Afghanistan, Mark shouldered his rucksack and walked into the gymnasium. Homemade posters and banners filled the space, all bearing the same message—welcome home.

In the past, he had bypassed this leg of the journey, knowing that no one would be waiting to greet him. He'd counted himself lucky to be spared the tears, never stopping to think about the joy he'd cut out of his life.

Today, for the first time, he navigated through the children and signs. He searched the unfamiliar faces and read the messages on their poster boards. Not one said his name. Maybe it had been too much to ask. Amy had a life at home. And he'd been adamant that she keep it—her kennel, her dogs, all of it.

It would prove challenging when he was stateside. He needed to be near the base. Picking up and moving to Oregon until he deployed again wasn't an option. But Amy seemed committed to making it work.

Talking about it over video chat and getting on a plane were two different things, however.

Woof! Woof!

Mark turned and spotted them. Rosie danced in circles at the end of her leash. Around her neck she wore a big yellow bow. He crossed to them, pushing his way through the crowd, needing to get to the beautiful blonde and the dog at her side. They were his family, his homecoming, everything he needed to feel loved in this world.

"Amy." Mark gathered her in his arms, holding her close. "You came."

"I've missed you so much," she whispered, her lips kissing his neck, his ear, anything she could reach. "Of course I came. I told you I'd be here."

He drew back and looked down into her eyes. "I wasn't sure if you could get away."

Months ago, when she'd told him she loved him, he'd believed her. He still did. But saying the words and making room in her life for him were two different things.

"Eloise can handle things for a while. I'm staying for as long as you're stateside. Rosie, too."

Mark dropped down on one knee to greet the puppy who had grown into a dog while he'd been away. Amy had sent pictures, but it wasn't the same. Rosie licked his face, scrambling to climb up onto his lap as if she didn't realize she wouldn't fit anymore. He'd hoped the dog would remember him, but he hadn't expected her joy.

"We should get out of here soon," Amy said. "I don't think dogs are allowed."

Mark stood, and Rosie pressed up against his legs as if she needed to touch him to know he was here and not a two-dimensional image. "I think they'll make an exception for her."

Amy moved toward him, and the tips of her black heels—wow, she'd worn heels for him—touched Rosie, who refused to give up her spot. Her hand brushed his cheek, a soft, suggestive caress. "I have a surprise for you."

Mark reached for her, drawing her as close as he could manage with the Belgian Malinois between them, and rested his forehead against hers. "I'm in. Whatever it is. I'm dying to make love to you, Amy. I want to dance with you until dawn."

"Then we really need to get out of here," she said, her voice low and husky.

"We'll need to find a hotel." He wished he'd taken the time to book something nice for her before he came home. But it had felt as if he was tempting fate. What if he booked a room for his homecoming and she bailed—or worse, he didn't make it back?

"No, we don't," she said. "I rented a house for us. It's nothing fancy, but it's near the base, and the owner agreed to let Rosie live there, too, for an extra deposit."

"We have a house?" He heard the awe in his voice.

"That's the surprise." She placed her hands flat against his chest, covering his thundering heart. "It's nothing fancy, and it's only temporary, but I wanted you to come back to a real home."

Mark stared down into her blue eyes—so damn beautiful, and all his. The emotions threatened to overwhelm him—awe, gratitude and, most of all, love.

"And it came furnished," she continued, running her hands down his chest, over his abdomen. If she kept going, he might be tempted to cause one hell of a scene. "There's a great big bed waiting for us."

Mark captured her wrists. "I hope you're wearing your lucky underwear."

"I might be."

"I can't wait to find out."

Wrapping one arm around Amy and holding Rosie's leash in his other hand, Mark led them to the exit. "Let's go home."

* * * * *

SPECIAL EXCERPT FROM

Blaze

Military veteran Mia Brandt agrees to a fake engagement to help sexy rescue swimmer Tag Johnson out of a jam. But could their fun, temporary liaison lead to something more?

Read on for a sneak preview at WICKED SECRETS by Anne Marsh, *part of our* ***UNIFORMLY HOT!*** *miniseries.*

Sailor boy didn't look up. Not because he didn't notice the other woman's departure—something about the way he held himself warned her he was aware of everyone and everything around him—but because polite clearly wasn't part of his daily repertoire.

Fine. She wasn't all that civilized herself.

The blonde made a face, her ponytail bobbing as she started hoofing it along the beach. "Good luck with that one," she muttered as she passed Mia.

Oookay. Maybe this *was* mission impossible. Still, she'd never failed when she'd been out in the field, and all her gals wanted was intel. She padded into the water, grateful for the cool soaking into her burning soles. The little things mattered so much more now.

"I'm not interested." Sailor boy didn't look up from the motor when she approached, a look of fierce concentration creasing his forehead. Having worked on more than one Apache helicopter during her two tours of duty, she knew the repair work wasn't rocket science.

HBEXP0315

She also knew the mechanic and…holy hotness.

Mentally, she ran through every curse word she'd learned. Tag Johnson hadn't changed much in five years. He'd acquired a few more fine lines around the corners of his eyes, possibly from laughing. Or from squinting into the sun since rescue swimmers spent plenty of time out at sea. The white scar on his forearm was as new as the lines, but otherwise he was just as gorgeous and every bit as annoying as he'd been the night she'd picked him up at the Star Bar in San Diego. He was also still out of her league, a military bad boy who was strong, silent, deadly…and always headed out the door.

For a brief second, she considered retreating. Unfortunately, the bridal party was watching her intently, clearly hoping she was about to score on their behalf. Disappointing them would be a shame.

"Funny," she drawled. "You could have fooled me."

Tag's head turned slowly toward her. Mia had hoped for drama. Possibly even his butt planting in the ocean from the surprise of her reappearance. No such luck.

"Sergeant Dominatrix," he drawled back.

HBEXP0315

HARLEQUIN®
A Romance FOR EVERY MOOD™